THE MARRIAGE ART
A New Approach to
Sexual Pleasure in Marriage

A DOCTOR SPEAKS:
"Dr. Eichenlaub's book is frank, complete and to the point. . . . The greater majority of books devoted to this subject go only so far in their approach and, because of propriety, shyness or some other reason, stop with the explanation and description only half given. . . . A post-graduate course for the married couple . . . without peer."
—*Richard R. Fliehr, M.D.*

A CLERGYMAN SPEAKS:
"I want to voice sincere appreciation for *The Marriage Art.* . . . I am certain that its direct and honest presentation will answer people's questions and meet their needs in this area of concern far better than any other book that I have read . . ."
—*The Reverend Frank Kroll*

THE
MARRIAGE
ART

by
John E. Eichenlaub, M.D.

A DELL BOOK

Published by
DELL PUBLISHING CO., INC.
1 Dag Hammarskjold Plaza
New York, N.Y. 10017
Copyright © 1961 by John E. Eichenlaub, M.D.
Dell ® TM 681510, Dell Publishing Co., Inc.

ISBN: 0-440-15422-7

Reprinted by arrangement with
Lyle Stuart, Inc., Secaucus, N.J. 07094
Printed in the U.S.A.
Previous Dell Edition #5422
New Dell Edition
First printing—August 1969
Second printing—June 1970
Third printing—September 1970
Fourth printing—January 1971
Fifth printing—April 1971
Sixth printing—January 1972
Seventh printing—December 1972
Eighth printing—May 1973
Ninth printing—November 1973
Tenth printing—February 1974
Eleventh printing—December 1974
Twelfth printing—September 1976
Thirteenth printing—July 1978

*This book exists because I see the married
couple as an ongoing team, as the biologic
unit which transcends the identity of
either husband or wife, and as the main
well-spring of life's gratifications.*

*My wife deserves much of the credit for
these ideas, and has thus earned the
gratitude of anyone who benefits from
this extension of them. I therefore
gratefully dedicate this book to*
BETTY R. EICHENLAUB

CONTENTS

THE MARRIAGE ART

Introduction:
Sex in Marriage

"Of course I believe in chastity!" one of my young associates said. "But I also believe in technique. I've seen too many couples who started off in sexual ignorance break up completely because of sexual dissatisfactions, or bicker continually because of sex-caused irritabilities and complications. The way it looks to me, you've got to choose the lesser of two evils: either you botch up a crucial part of your marriage from lack of experience, or you throw out the ideal of sex as a ritual of love-union, shared only between husband and wife."

Right at that moment, I decided to write this book. Because there *is* a third way: a way to cleave to each other as man and wife without blundering along in total ignorance. You can read about the facts and techniques you need for sexual success and work them out *as a couple* inside the bounds of marriage.

THE MARRIAGE ART was specifically designed for such couple use. Whether you have been married for many years or are just preparing for the connubial state, this book offers several distinctive features:

This book tells you what you need to know all the way from start to finish.

Most books take you right up to the point of sexual union, then leave you to bungle along unguided just when you need help the most. This book carries you from the first stirring of sexual impulse to the final culmination and afterglow in absolutely complete detail. It pays particular attention to the moments of advanced intimacy and actual union with which most couples have the least experience before marriage and have the most trouble getting guidance.

This book helps you as a couple.

The older works on sex instruct the man, and leave him to control the woman. That might have worked when Father ruled with an iron hand and Mother meekly followed. However, today's women have not been reared to do exactly as their husbands tell them. Today's men neither have nor want total responsibility for crucial family and couple affairs. Modern couples approach mutual problems by mutual endeavor. They determine the household budget, policies for child training, choice of vacations and dozens of other issues *together,* not on the basis of male dominance. To make sex an exception imposes strange and unacceptable roles upon both parties and seriously disturbs their relationship just when it should be at its closest.

This book avoids this error, and lets you build *together* in commencing or improving your sex life. Both husbands and wives learn their duties and responsibilities in establishing and improving sexual communion and in solving various couple problems.

This book views couple problems constructively.

You can blame most of the difficulties which couples face upon one party if you wish. However, this practice sets the stage for arguments, recriminations and guilt instead of for progress. If the man reaches his climax before the woman feels content, you can follow the ancient, erroneous views: blame him for poor control, blame her for a cold nature, or blame both. No matter which course you follow, nothing constructive results.

This book's couple viewpoint usually proves much more helpful. When you view the problem as one of couple harmony, both parties can work toward improvement. You can definitely enhance feminine ardor and ease biologic pressures on the male if you forget worthless arguments about blame and attack your problem *as a team.* This book tells you exactly how to remedy the common couple problems with constructive, easily managed couple techniques, and how to end once and for all the vicious circle of guilt, recrimination, and couple conflict creating emotional disturbance and sexual failure, which in turn calls forth more guilt, recrimination and couple conflict.

This book helps you at every stage of sexual achievement.

Whether you want to get your sex life off to a sound start, redeem it after years of frequent failure and halfway success, or improve it in spite of reasonable satisfaction, this book offers specific and worthwhile help.

As beginners, you will find specific directions for dealing with the virginal membrane and specific techniques for building sexual excitement in a woman who has not yet developed full sexual sensitivity or responsiveness. You will find detailed methods for assuring the bride's comfort during early sexual episodes and for maintaining good couple control. You will find certain sex positions recommended for technical ease and unstrained alignment of organs.

If sexual failures or inadequacies plague you, this book tells exactly how to rebuild mutual attraction and rid yourselves of emotional tangles and domestic problems. It details positions and techniques which take advantage of sexually sensitive areas found only in experienced women. It takes up problems and difficulties which may have kept you from pleasing each other adequately, including childbirth-stretched vagina, excessively fast male climax, lack of feminine fervor and disparity between the husband's and wife's desire.

If you want to improve upon an already good sex life, this book suggests literally dozens of caresses suitable to every stage of the proceedings, at least a few of which will add variety and excitement to your encounters. It shows how birth control techniques which did not interfere with satisfaction early in marriage could be real barriers to full sexual enjoyment *now*, and suggests alternative methods. It describes exercises and techniques which enhance your capacities to please each other, increase your power to have relations often, and boost some episodes to exquisite heights. You will learn how to keep sex from becoming stale, how to give your partner extra thrills in special celebration-sex events, how to keep your adjustment undamaged through prolonged illnesses, pregnancies and other sexual constraints.

You can use this book at any stage of your sexual adjustment. In fact, most couples will profit from reading it over and over as their sexual situation changes through the years.

This book sticks to its subject.

Every word in this book has to do with sexual satisfaction in marriage. Although some material on the anatomy and physiology of sexual satisfaction and the influence of your emotional adjustment and household arrangements upon sex is included, anatomy, physiology and sociology are considered only insofar as they affect sexual satisfaction. If you want further information on these matters, you can find excellent advice in the textbooks used in preparation for marriage or in marriage and family life courses. (For instance, your library might supply Clifford H. Adams' book, PREPARING FOR MARRIAGE; Evelyn Millis Duvall and Reuben Hill's WHEN YOU MARRY; or Judson T. and Mary G. Landis' BUILDING A SUCCESSFUL MARRIAGE.)

THE MARRIAGE ART centers entirely on the sexual side of marriage instead of trying to help with all aspects of domestic adjustment.

This book presents facts and techniques in a logical, easily understood order.

THE MARRIAGE ART provides an introductory summary of background material, followed by instruction in managing each stage of a sexual episode. Chapters Seven through Twelve amount to a trouble-shooting manual and guide to further refinements. This organization makes the material easy to follow and to understand and helps you to find guidance on any problems which arise over the years.

This book ends with a step-by-step program for successfully commencing, redeeming or improving sexual communion.

The organization of basic material according to the various stages of the love-union and the common problems involved in sex inevitably mixes some techniques and methods suited only to experienced and accomplished couples in with its fundamentals. Chapter Twelve gives a step-by-step program for commencing or redeeming satisfactory sexual adjustment and for going on to keenly developed sexual skill. This chapter tells you exactly what to do at each stage, directing you to the pertinent passages in the rest of the book for details. You can glance at this chapter any time you want suggestions for further progress toward improved couple communion, or reread it at intervals to remind you of ideas suitable for the stage of adjustment which you have attained.

Read it together, read it apart.

You may want to discuss sex technique item by item to improve your couple approach. You may want to read this material chapter by chapter, then discuss its content at a later date. You may want to read it separately and apply its ideas directly during sexual exchange. Use whatever approach suits your own attitudes and relationship. No matter how you use it, you will find material which defines *couple* action to combat *couple* problems and to achieve *couple* satisfaction a real asset to your marital communion. You can undoubtedly build a better sex life *together* with aid and guidance from this book.

1.
How
Sexual Satisfaction
Comes About

From the first fundamentals of satisfactory union to the most masterful variations of the sexually adept, all sex technique is based on the same pattern of physical and emotional response. The pattern starts with a framework which makes sexual abandonment possible, moves on through stirrings of sex interest to the step-by-step build-up of sexual excitement, and ends with a peace-bringing climax or recession of feeling. You can please each other much more thoroughly and consistently if you build your sex technique on an understanding of these facts.

Framework for sexual union.

Besides physical manipulations, marital communion involves emotional interplay. Many factors exert influence over sexual capacities. You need to provide a proper emotional and situational framework for sex in order to achieve successful marital communion. Some of the most vexing sexual problems respond to simple attentions in this sphere.

You do not have to be "in the mood for sex" before

your partner can bestir your interest, but you do have to be in a passably cheerful emotional state. Even if the emotional aspect of connubial sex meant nothing, the physical processes themselves involve nerve pathways which any major emotional disturbance thoroughly blocks. Depression, anger, fear or tension affect the muscles and glands of your sexual apparatus in ways which make successful sexual communion nearly impossible. Only a calm or happy emotional state leaves every needed nerve fiber free for its sexual function.

A great deal of sexual excitement and satisfaction stems from emotional echoes and re-echoes. When you feel very close to each other, you respond compassionately to your partner's feelings and he responds to yours, building excitement in ever broader spirals. A barrier of reserve or ill-feeling between you blankets these responses, leaving sex a poor process of mechanical relief.

You must abandon yourself in uninhibited sexual indulgence to savor its full measure. Lingering doubts as to the propriety of sex itself, or of sexual practices in which you might engage, act as strong dampers to excitement and release. Doubts as to the propriety of sex at any particular moment because of lack of privacy or other such concerns may also restrain your sexual response.

Physical attraction through sight, sound and smell.

Sexual excitement begins with general attraction. A man looks at his wife, and something in her posture, in her facial expression, or in her movements suddenly reminds him of the special womanly appeal which she holds for him. Sometimes sound or smell conveys appeal: her tone of voice, her perfume or certain natural scents arouse his male interest. Women respond to comparable manly attractions, such as muscular strength or forthright behavior.

At the moment, perhaps nothing further happens. A gentle pat or brushing kiss satisfies both parties. But the first stirring of sexual desire has been felt; and, with encouragement, it soon becomes an avalanche.

In the past, many people have mistakenly thought of the first stirrings of sexual desire as spontaneous. Need for sexual relief and craving for sexual pleasures definitely arise in most men and in many women, often making them quite susceptible to allurement. However, attraction toward a partner by sight, sound and smell usually must whet sexual appetites before excitement will build up. Measures aimed at preserving or heightening your biological appeal definitely help to increase the "spontaneous" stirring of the sex impulse.

Conditioning plays a big part in marital allurement. The remnants and memories of past success increase each partner's attraction for the other. If a given scent, nightdress or overture has always been associated with unusual sexual delights, it subtly bestirs excitement later on. The sense of smell seems especially apt for subtle allurement, perhaps because couples can enjoy its presence throughout a sexual encounter. A soft, pink boudoir light, a bedtime glass of wine or a special passion-signifying negligee may serve to reinforce allurement, especially if you make a point of using them only when you are certain of an unusually satisfying union. Of course, conditioning can also play a negative role: a husband who lets his advances become linked with pain or fear in his wife's mind creates a barrier which may last for weeks or months. But most couples can build a substantial backlog of pleasant sexual experience, with many specific associations of scents, garments, scene-settings or rituals with highly gratifying sex.

Sex sensitivity through touch.

Even though vision, hearing and smell continue to contribute toward sexual excitement, the build-up of intense passion soon requires contact and caress. At this stage, the guiding principle is that *gentle stroking and caress (perhaps made even gentler by moisture or lubrication) build excitement best until the last big push to climax*. The nerves which build sub-climactic sexual excitement are light-touch nerves, not pressure or pain nerves. Firmer types of preliminary caress work well only on body structures whose sexually excitable elements lie deep beneath the skin, such as the nipple and certain portions of the genitals. Otherwise, a silky touch proves more exciting.

When you and your mate set out to bring your sex pace into harmony, it is a key point that your own caresses can stimulate *you* as well as your partner through the effect of bodily contact on sexually-alive touch nerves. The palms of your hands are very much alive sexually, while the tips of your fingers are not. Any caress or bodily contact involving the moist inner surface of your lips or the tip of your tongue builds your own excitement as well as your partner's, while rolled-in lips or the center of your tongue have little sexual sensitivity. What you caress *with* and what *you* caress have as much to do with sex pace as what your partner caresses, at the same time affording him or her (after a little experience) with a delicate index of your needs and desires.

Many sexually-alive body areas respond mainly to your partner's caress rather than to contact brought on through your own activity. Women depend especially heavily on passion-building caress of parts other than the genitals, such as the hair, the ear lobes, the sides of the neck, the upper arm, the breast, the low back, the buttocks and the inner thigh. The breasts have two different sorts of sexual sensitivity: surface sensitivity like that of other trigger spots, and special sensitivity centered in the milk ducts just behind the nipple. Sexual sensitivity in men centers more in the back and less in the breast area, and has less importance by comparison with the hands, mouth and genitals than in the female.

Genital sensitivity.

Young ladies who have not yet indulged in sex play or activity have sexual sensitivity in only one part of their genital apparatus: the clitoris, which is located in the folds just in front of the vaginal outlet. The clitoris remains soft and difficult to identify until a woman's ardor is aroused; it stands out like a firm little pencil stub when sexual excitement is high.

After several months of frequent connubial success, a woman's areas of sexual sensitivity change. (The extent of this change is proved by the fact that sexual responsiveness never develops if the clitoris is surgically removed beforehand; sexual sensitivity remains unimpaired if this organ is removed after sexual adjustment has been accomplished.) The inner lips at the vaginal outlet, the vagina itself, and even the urinary passage just in front of the vagina (which is caught and rubbed between the penis and the pelvic bone during intercourse) become keenly sensitive. Thus the clitoris is the main touch-button of sensual delight in early marriage, but only one of many such touch-buttons in a woman with well-nurtured responsiveness.

In men, gentle touch upon the scrotal sac and the top surface of the penis build keen (but not climactic) sexual excitement. The rim of the penile head contains keenly sensitive nerves, especially at the bottom-surface corner where a small membrane called the frenulum attaches.

Natural lubrication.

When a woman becomes sexually aroused, glands in and around the vagina make a mildly lubricating juice. Unfortunately, this juice tends to remain within the vagina itself, at least until the changes which follow childbirth relax the vaginal outlet. The tissues at the vaginal opening (especially the two inner folds just in front of the vagina) badly need lubrication both to make caresses feel stimulatingly silky and to prevent discomfort during or after intercourse. Ordinarily, the husband can use the moist vagina as a source for lubricant, transferring female juice to the surface with dip-and-stroke caresses several times during genital play. With a new bride or a woman who has had too little sexual satisfaction in the past to make anticipation awaken her glandular responses, artificial lubricants prove quite helpful.

The male sex organ puts out a little lubricating fluid. The glands which make this fluid line the inside of the urinary tube. Ordinarily, most or all of the fluid remains inside instead of working its way to the surface. If a deficiency of natural lubrication impairs your sex life, this sometimes proves a useful source of extra lubrication. Either the man or the woman can easily strip out and spread this fluid just before intercourse begins.

The near-climactic and climactic shifts.

When sexual excitement reaches its ultimate peak, touch-type stimulation no longer has much effect. The key parts of both the male and female sex organs do not even have nerve fibers to carry the gentler types of skin sensitivity (light touch, deep touch, and coolness). They have only pain- and heat-sensitive nerve ends. Climactic caresses in other areas best mimic and add impetus to genital stimulation when they also bring pain fibers into play. Muscle clutching, pinching, slapping and biting stimulate the same nerve type exactly as genital friction, and broaden the basis for the climactic surge. This can be done without roughness or brutality, as the chapters on specific techniques will show, but calls for much different caresses than the earlier stage of sex play.

External genital contact.

Most nerve centers contributing to sexual excitement lie near the vaginal opening in the female and around the penile head in the male. Sexual frictions without deep penetration can thus contribute greatly to sexual excitement before you enter the final surge to tranquilization and subsidence. The head of the penis fits snugly within the moist outer lips of the female organ, bringing both partners' most sexually sensitive areas into play. This situation is especially apt when the wife has had little experience or gratification in the past, so that sexual sensitivity in her genitals still centers sharply in the clitoris. External genital contact permits considerable friction of the penis against the clitoris, which can otherwise only be achieved with deep penetration, and it does not push the husband toward an early climax as strongly as deep penetration does.

Complete genital contact.

During actual intercourse, a couple derives some sexual stimulation from merely lying together in snug sexual contact even if there is no movement at all. In and out motions rub the shaft of the penis to and fro against the sensitive structures at the vaginal opening and press the tip of the penis against the vaginal wall (mainly the front surface of that wall in most sex positions). Either the man or the woman can produce considerable friction of the shaft of the penis against the clitoris by sidewise lunging or rolling motions in certain positions. This helps to build female excitement without speeding the male climax. Considerable sexual stimulation also comes from motion of and pressure upon sexually sensitive parts, which are entirely different forms of stimulation from friction. Thus a man can evoke gratifying responses in his wife by twitching the deeply inserted penis even though no rubbing of sex parts occurs.

Movement of the genitals independent of other body motions calls for considerable training and effort, but helps many couples to new heights of sexual success. Like the muscles with which you keep urination under control, these muscles carry out their tasks involuntarily and beyond range of conscious control unless you deliberately train yourself to govern their functioning. When a wife learns to control her vaginal muscles, she can improve the couple's sex life even without exer-

cising her newly found capacities during the sex act
itself: by periodically contracting her vagina, she can
build up the muscular strength of that organ and make
for snugger and more active sexual union. If her control becomes sufficient to permit voluntary waves and
twitches during sexual contact, enrichment of both
her own and her partner's sexual gratification can
result. Some women, after several years' experience,
become sufficiently adept at vaginal contraction to
use it even during a sex climax without giving unduly
distracting thought to the process.

Different and separate actions result from lifting-
type contractions: trying to draw the vaginal opening
straight up into your body or trying to pull the rectal
opening inward. With practice, many women become
quite adept at such motions, adding considerable
variety to their sexual activities.

Male genital movement is limited to twitchings
transmitted from the muscles just behind the scrotum.
These muscles surround the two stiffening roots of the
penis. When the penis becomes rigid during sexual
excitement, muscular contraction in this area moves
the entire organ in short, sharp arcs. If you try to lift
the back margin of the scrotum straight up into your
body, these muscles will contract. When the penis is
erect, its tip will jog perhaps a half inch. This motion
is entirely independent of other bodily actions, and
with a little practice can be performed either in rapid
runs of two or three per second, rhythmically during
the interval between penetration and withdrawal on
each sex stroke, and in several other pleasant variations
on ordinary sexual friction.

Male orgasm.

At the climax of male sexual excitement and activity, a series of rhythmic spasms in the muscles at the base of the penis set that organ twitching and expel a jetlike stream of sperm-containing liquid. These phenomena result from overwhelming activity in the parasympathetic nerves, which ordinarily govern body functions in tranquility and oppose or quell the type of nervous activity associated with excitement or upset. Complete release from sexual excitement and a blissful sense of repose generally follow the orgasm.

For a few moments before the orgasm, a man's whole being becomes the rampant slave of reproductive instinct. The primitive pain nerves throughout his body become sexual triggers ready and waiting for his partner's slapping, scratching, squeeze or bite. His muscles only want release from voluntary self-control to bound into sex motions without plan or deliberation. This is the moment when anything goes; because the meanest, roughest feminine assault only heightens a husband's sensual delight.

A few seconds later, the quieting fertile surge requires entirely different cooperation. Gentle containment, sweet caress and the rapturous kiss add to the soothing release which spreads through the husband's body.

The twitchings and jetstream of the male orgasm stimulate the female partner toward a sexual climax. In some women, this source of gratification is so important that methods of birth control which interfere with the impact of semen on the vaginal wall greatly impair sexual satisfaction.

Female orgasm.

At the ultimate climax of sexual excitement, paroxysms of muscular movement often occur in a woman's vagina, accompanied by a sense of intense sexual transportation. In many women, such an orgastic climax almost always accompanies complete satisfaction after full sexual awakening. Others receive perfectly adequate gratification from sex without having orgasm. A few women require a series of orgasms to feel replete.

Non-orgastic satisfaction.

A feeling of physical repose follows any natural and complete subsidence of sexual excitement. A definite feeling of self-satisfaction generally follows when you have demonstrated your capacity to please your partner. Many women find these gratifications quite sufficient to make sex a wonderful part of their married life even without orgasmic release. Certainly some episodes without mutual orgasm occur in all marriages. With proper management to assure gradual and complete subsidence (since no willing sex partner should ever be left dangling in a state of undissipated excitement), these can contribute materially to the marital satisfactions.

A few episodes in which the husband allows his excitement to subside gradually instead of passing through the final surge also have worthwhile advantages for some couples. Such episodes give considerable low-key sexual satisfaction to both husband and wife without in any way decreasing capacity for later orgasm-climaxed episodes, and they sometimes act as a potent energizing and masculinity-building tonic. And they afford priceless training in couple control, through which many couples learn how to pace their sexual crescendos for keenly mutual orgastic climaxes in later sexual communions.

Most people require a prolonged period of gradually subsiding afterplay to dissipate sexual tension without going through an orgasm. Close body contact without genital movement or friction helps to quiet sexual excitement. Whispers of endearment and gratitude help reinforce the feeling of sexual capability which is such an important part of non-orgastic satisfaction. In a sense, the mind and emotions soothe the body instead of vice versa. Even if one partner has had the more rapidly satisfying form of release, continued tapering love play is a crucial part of successful couple union if either needs further quietude.

Fertility.

A couple can make pregnancy somewhat more or somewhat less likely by timing their sexual encounters. A woman's ovaries ordinarily produce no more than one egg cell in each menstrual month, about fourteen days before the beginning of her flow. The most fertile period lasts from two days before ovulation (since sperm can survive two days) until three days after (when the egg cell generally dies). Couples who want to postpone pregnancy by the rhythm method generally avoid intercourse for two days on each side of the most fertile period, or from the ninth to the nineteenth day if the woman has a regular twenty-eight-day cycle. For a woman with a twenty-nine-day cycle, the unsafe period is one day later (tenth to twentieth day), for a thirty-day-cycle the unsafe period runs from the eleventh to the twenty-first day, and so on.

The rhythm method of decreasing pregnancies only cuts the normal reproductive rate slightly more than half, so that couples who have no religious scruples against chemical or mechanical methods usually prefer one of the techniques described in Chapter Seven of this book. Timing relations to conform to the most fertile period definitely helps you to have babies more promptly when you want to reproduce though.

Some couples interrupt sexual intercourse at the last possible moment as a means of attempting to make pregnancy unlikely. Besides decreasing the satisfaction of sex life markedly for both parties, this method is really quite ineffective. The preliminary lubricating fluids made by the male sex organ carry enough sperm to cause pregnancy fairly frequently, and the split-second timing required to prevent any semen from being discharged within the vagina seldom proves reliable through the years.

Certain sex positions have frequently been held to be more fertile than others, because they deposit the sperm closer to the mouth of the womb. Considering the muscular motions and frictions of the sexual climax, this element probably has very little to do with the outcome in any ordinary sexual posture. However, a position which places the woman on her knees with her chest lowered to the surface of the bed and her husband approaching from behind has certain pregnancy-promoting features. In this posture, a displaced uterus often drops into a highly receptive position. Moreover, the semen tends to puddle right at the mouth of the womb (through which the sperm must find their way if pregnancy is to occur). This effect can be accentuated by lying on the abdomen for a few minutes after intercourse. Several of my patients who had previously seemed unable to conceive became pregnant after adopting this method.

As long as one or more episodes fall inside the most fertile period, the frequency of sexual relations probably has little effect on the likelihood of pregnancy. In a few couples, extremely frequent intercourse keeps the sperm from maturing properly (which takes about three days) and fertility actually increases when frequency of intercourse is cut. The female orgasm has nothing to do with fertility, since the muscular movements involved have no effect on the deposition and movement of sperm. Neither frequency of sex relations nor feminine orgasm has anything to do with the conception of twins.

Summary of essential background for sexual technique.

The blessings of successful sexual communion stem from an intensive build-up of sexual excitement, followed by satisfactory dissipation thereof. Since all strong emotions use the same sets of nerve fibers, your mood and circumstances affect your sexual capacities greatly. Your individual attitudes toward sex and your personal relationship with each other contribute strongly toward sexual success or failure. Good grooming and simple allurement help to encourage sexual interest. Conditioning also plays its part. Once sexual interest is aroused, gentle stroking and caress (perhaps made even gentler by moisture or lubrication) builds excitement. What you caress *with* builds sexual excitement as well as what your partner caresses, but women especially depend on stimulation of parts other than the genitals to build sexual excitement. Early in marriage, caressing of the female genitalia must concentrate on the clitoris. Several other structures around the vaginal opening become sexually sensitive after sexual awakening. Deliberate transfer of the natural fluids from within the female reservoir to the sensitive outer surfaces usually provides needed lubrication. The nerve fibers stimulated in the final surge to orgastic climax resemble pain rather than touch, making the nip, the pinch, the muscle clutch and extra firm friction effective supplements. A phase of superficial genital friction excites both partners very effectively without spurring the man toward too quick a climax. Several varieties of friction, contact and movement enliven sexual intercourse itself, many of them very effective in gratifying one or the other partner (or both). The male orgasm involves muscle twitching and emission of fluid jets which contribute considerably to female gratification. Female orgasm also involves rhythmic spasms in the genital musculature and brings almost immediate sexual repose. Gradual subsidence of sexual excitement can permit a woman considerable satisfaction without orgasm. Timing of sexual activity influences the chance of pregnancy somewhat. Fertility usually need not affect your choice of sex position, and remains unaffected by frequency of relations or of feminine orgasm.

2.
The First Key to
Soundly Satisfying Sex:
Attraction and Appeal

Let's begin at the beginning, with the earliest stages of sexual attraction. As you go about your everyday married life, sexual impulses and responsiveness build up. Perhaps they take days or weeks to reach the level at which you consciously recognize them. Perhaps they remain beneath the conscious level all the time, only emerging when your partner stirs them up. But sexual allurement builds or wanes in every moment which you spend together. Sex is not a thing apart from daily married life: it is the final yielding to allurement deliberately or unintentionally exerted day by day, hour by hour, and minute by minute.

A wife cannot loaf around the house in slovenly and unattractive garb, screech at the children all through every evening, and sleep in curlers six nights in a row, then expect to overcome a week of half-repulsion in a few minutes of deliberate appeal. A husband cannot expect to speak gruffly, bathe infrequently, and strew his clothes around the bedroom, then inspire wifely response with a few quick caresses.

You and your wife or husband presumably have positive appeal for each other. Only distinct and mutual attraction leads to courtship and marriage in our society. You do not need artifice in exerting sex appeal. You need only to keep your partner's sensibilities in mind, and give them due regard.

The simple points of personal grooming should receive careful attention. A shower or shave may help you to rouse your wife's ardor more than any caress. A soft, clean nightgown may inspire your husband to unmatched passion. Pleasantly scented grooming aids for men, and perfume or Eau de Cologne for women, serve not only as simple allurements, but also as elements in erotogenic conditioning—the frequent association of a given scent with pleasant intimacies ultimately makes that scent itself exciting. Recently popularized bath oils such as Sardo impart a youthful and pleasant feel to the skin which generally enhances a woman's attractiveness for her husband, too.

Your physical appeal lays crucial groundwork for sexual excitement long before either you or your partner starts to plan for a connubial encounter. Minute by minute, hour by hour, you build the partnership urge. Build it as thoroughly and consistently as possible!

Sexual by-play.

Allurement ultimately leads to a sex impulse in one or the other of you, whereupon deliberate sexual overtures and knowing response replace the vaguer types of appeal. These early overtures should build preliminary excitement and help to keep the impulse alive until the proper occasion for intercourse arrives, but should not drive you toward rushed or inappropriate communion. An ardent spur-of-the-moment tumble sounds very romantic, especially when a few casually conceived kisses reveal previously unsuspected, keenly mutual desire. However, ineptly arranged intercourse leaves the clothes you had no chance to shed in a shambles, your plans for the evening shot, your birth control program incomplete, and your future sex play under considerable better-be-careful-or-we'll-wind-up-in-bed-again restraint. Best keep your by-play mild until you know that further sexual activity will not stir later regrets.

Hints and private signals.

Awareness that sex is in the offing usually starts through words and gestures. You can promote this process without interfering with spontaneity by developing a few pet terms or signals which express your interest or desires. Think of your partner's physical attractions for you, and make a point of referring to these sexual assets during sex play and participation. After a husband has complimented "the smoothest skin this side of Heaven" while he strokes it in passionate embrace, nicknames like "Velvet" take on new meaning. After a wife has called her husband "Muscles" as she squeezes his naked thigh, a significant pressure on his biceps can boost his sex urge. Private endearments which express appreciation and respect for your partner's sexual qualities also have great value. Try calling your wife an "A-1 tumblebun" or your husband a "great big hunk of wonderful man" when you're obviously moving toward a sexual encounter, or when you have just enjoyed a successful communion. You can also open a considerable horizon for enticing references to sex by having your own private word or words for it. One couple calls their sex life "sport" for instance. The by-play of subtle enticement which goes on when they discuss their sporting life and mood at social gatherings lends an excitement to their verbal preliminaries like that of a courting couple's stolen kiss.

Availability.

If you want good sex adjustment as a couple, you must have sexual relations approximately as often as the man requires. This does not mean that you have to jump into bed if he gets the urge in the middle of supper or when you are dressing for a big party. But it does mean that a woman should never turn down her husband on appropriate occasions simply because she has no yearning of her own for sex or because she is tired or sleepy, or indeed for any reason short of a genuine disability. As a rule of thumb, I usually tell women *always* to meet their husbands' sexual requirements unless frank disability keeps them from performing their usual household or working duties or specific disorders of the sex organs themselves make intercourse impossible. Sex is too important for any wife to give it less call upon her energy than cooking, laundry, and a dozen other activities.

In our culture, most couples do not engage in sexual intercourse during the menstrual flow. However, menstruation need not prohibit sexual relations entirely. Any question as to whether the period is normal or whether bleeding might stem from miscarriage should interdict intercourse (and also the use of internal feminine protection, tub baths, or any other measure which might move ever-present germs up the vagina). Menstruation limits the variety of preliminary caresses somewhat and makes sex too messy for many fastidious men and women. Even with disposable plastic-backed bed pads (from the hospital or sickroom supplies counter of your drugstore) sex during the menstrual flow makes for lots of laundry. However, many couples find that the wife can be quite easily aroused during the latter days of the menstrual flow, and that neither party objects to the mess. Certainly, there is no medical reason to omit sex during menstrual flow in times of extreme and reciprocal ardor.

Aside from the menstrual holidays, which you should observe if either of you so desire, constant availability makes sense in several different ways. The wife who always searches herself to see whether passion is developing only builds sexual anxieties which impair or actually wreck her responsiveness. Constant availability builds your wifely appeal because every sexual impulse is nourished by the memory of past successes and is not impaired by the memory of sexual rebuffs. It builds your husband's sexual capabilities, too, because total confidence and certainty that sexual activity will never lead to disappointment is the most effective potency builder known to man. Even if you have to settle for only occasional episodes in which the wife gains total orgasmic satisfaction (and many couples do), the other episodes help the wife as well as the husband by keeping the pressure of pent-up sexual desire from pushing him into a mutually unsatisfactory quick climax on those occasions when her passion does run high.

Although orgasm gives the ultimate in sexual reward, I have known women who never had an orgasm and yet regarded sex as a great personal satisfaction. Pleasing someone you love and meeting biologic needs competently with your body brings full contentment to many women during non-climactic sexual intercourse, just as nursing a baby brings contentment to a willing mother. If anything, non-climactic sex is easier to enjoy than nursing, since a considerate husband can always make intercourse comfortable while even a well-meaning infant sometimes bites. If you conscientiously work at being available, you may ultimately find the feminine role quite satisfying even in the absence of ardor or desire.

Although fairness would seem to dictate similar efforts to please by husbands whose wives require extra gratifications, the male can perform sexually only when he is sufficiently aroused to permit erection. He cannot match her in availability and should not try; but he can help to meet his wife's requirements in several other ways, as discussed in later chapters.

Preliminary caresses.

A woman's hair and earlobes, upper arms, back, breasts and several other areas respond actively to her husband's light caress. Probably the keenest trigger to early masculine sex interest is the palm of the hand. Some wives stroke this area when they feel particularly interested in sex, others encourage its use in male-originated sex play when their own ardor makes it safe to accelerate their swain's excitement. Certainly, both partners should remember that *a man who strokes sexually sensitive areas with his fingertips usually builds his wife's excitement faster than his own, while a man who strokes gently with his palm, kisses softly or titillates with his tongue builds his own excitement at least as much as his mate's.* A woman also can increase her own rate of excitement by pressing her sexually sensitive areas against her mate during a responsive embrace, by placing her husband's hand upon response-triggering sites, or by clutching or kneading caresses of his back or thigh.

Teasing and coquetry.

The game of advance and retreat undoubtedly plays an important part in building sexual excitement. However, teasing and coquetry in the early stages of sexual by-play have a highly limited place in marriage. Until sex play has progressed far enough to assure both parties that it *is* play and not hesitation, teasing and coquetry often seem perilously close to rejection. The emotional security and faith in your own sexual attractiveness which come from your partner's constant willingness to fulfill your needs mean a great deal. Your partner should not impair your self-confidence and your faith in your loving relationship by excessive teasing, and you should also avoid this error. Both of you should express your sexual interest and desires forthrightly instead of deliberately suppressing them in teasing or coquettish retreat, especially in the first few months of your sexual adjustment or readjustment. As a rule of thumb, I would say:

¶ When you first try coquetry or teasing wait until you are actually in bed together and well along with sexual preliminaries, so that your partner cannot possibly doubt that your teasing is part of your effort to please rather than a threatened withdrawal.

¶ Confine teasing and coquetry to the latter period of sexual by-play, after your behavior entirely establishes your intention of acceding to your partner's wishes, for at least six months.

¶ Always stop teasing immediately if your partner shows signs of being upset and anxious instead of stimulated by your devices.

Practical applications of Chapter Two.

Sexual impulses and responsiveness arise through attractions for each other which you can deliberately cultivate. When the first gambits of sexual by-play show that your partner's ardor is beginning to rise, suggestive or mildly exciting gestures and private allusions help you to keep the urge alive until a suitable occasion for sex arrives. *Never think of sexual by-play or early sexual caresses as tentative approaches by which the husband explores his wife's willingness to go on.* She should *always* be willing to go on. Her husband's confidence in his sexual attraction and in marriage as perpetual consent (which both the law and religion affirm it to be) mean more both to him and to her than the enhanced ardor she might derive if only approached when in the grips of passion. You should confine teasing and coquetry to circumstances and techniques which raise no question of true rejection or denial.

3.
The Second Key to
Soundly Satisfying Sex:
Sex Play

When you know that you can continue a sexual episode to its destined conclusion if the urge develops, the restraints of sexual by-play fall away. You can caress each other freely without concern for building too much ardor. Intercourse will not necessarily result; some couples enjoy gradually mounting waves of sexual interest and excitement for several days before they reach that climax. But the fact that passion can completely rule your acts opens a broad vista of caress and interplay.

Sex play brings vast delight to most couples in itself. You should explore its pleasures fully. However, it also contributes greatly to the success of the sexual communion which follows. Ideal preliminary play fills you with expanding, captivating, delightfully exciting love. Only on this foundation can the finest episodes of connubial bliss be built.

You can explore many varieties of mouth-to-mouth play in the course of a sexual encounter. Closed-mouth kissing with various degrees of pressure, with moist lips or with dry, with light brushing contact or with various motions, all yield pleasurable and exciting sensations under certain circumstances. Open-mouth play can be a momentary break in closed-mouth activity: just as her husband presses his lips to hers, the wife bares her teeth and opens her mouth to give him a gentle, unexpected nip, then as he draws back she ardently presses her moist warm lips to his. After sexual excitement has become intense, a more prolonged interval of open-mouth play may build it further: both partners intermittently press their parted lips together, groping for sensitive spots with their tongue-tips and nipping gently at each other's lips and tongue.

Petting and embrace offer many ways of building sexual excitement and of keeping freshness and variety in your sex play. *From the time your ardor first becomes aroused until the last whispered compliment before you say good night, your hands should rarely or never be entirely still.* Man or woman, you should stroke, caress and embrace your partner in never-ceasing physical expression of your endearment, your excitement, and your fervid release.

Useful caresses.

You will usually find that *rhythmic stroking caresses* stir early sexual excitement most intensely. You can stroke the ears and ear lobes, hair, shoulders, arms and hands, inner thighs, breast area, lower abdomen, back and buttocks. Stroke through clothing at first, then shift to bare-skin contact as sexual arousal progresses. Sometimes a preliminary bath with bath oil or a light dusting with powder makes your skin more pleasant to stroke and enhances your responsiveness to caress.

Although most women respond much more keenly than men to gentle stroking and almost require this type of preliminary play to become fully aroused, husbands also welcome this type of caress. Remember the general principle that stroking with the whole hand generally proves exciting to both parties, while finger-tip stroking usually excites the passive partner more than the active one.

Playful *tweaks and jiggles* lend pleasant variety, freshness and surprise to your early love play. Pain-pinches and nips fit in only at a much later stage, if at all, but a sudden, unexpected stimulation gives excitement quite a boost in any phase of the proceedings.

After you have both become moderately aroused, somewhat deeper-lying nerve fibers produce added excitement. Try bunching your fingertips together. Press them into a sexually sensitive but reasonably lean area, such as the back or the lower abdomen, and move them back and forth or in a circle as far as the skin will readily stretch. In plumper areas such as the buttocks or thighs, pick up a fold of tissue between your thumb and fingers and use the same motions for stimulation. Do not pinch the skin painfully: only grasp it firmly enough to stimulate the deeper nerves.

Besides this form of finger-tip caress, most wives find similar pressures and motions, applied with the fingers separated and partially clawed, helpful in stimulating their husbands' upper backs and chests. This caress works especially well in maintaining and building a husband's excitement during periods of mouth-to-breast and mouth-to-body types of play. Time after time, I have seen women who complain of inadequate preparation before intercourse whose husbands jump from a few kisses to fast insertion of the penis for no other reason than fear of losing erection. The woman blames the man for neglect, the man doubts his own potency and control, and neither gets much satisfaction out of sex. Viewed as *individual* problems, the difficulties seem insoluble. Viewed as a *couple* problem, the difficulties almost always disappear. Once the woman recognizes her responsibility for maintaining her husband's excitement she can easily keep his erection firm and secure for many minutes, leaving him free to stimulate her in new and delightful ways. By working as a couple they can prolong precoital play to fulfill both parties' fond desires.

When sexual excitement has built up, strong, deep muscle-clutching caresses may stir a final surge. "Horse bite" clutching of the thighs or buttocks, fist-pounding on the upper back and other wantonly harsh actions lend still further joy when excitement runs high. Even such cat-like meanness as raking your husband's chest with your long nails may heighten ardor when the time is ripe. Anything short of actual injury is quite proper in moments of keenest ardor. Harsh caresses fit intense excitement only, though, and should be saved for moments of overwhelming passion.

One form of deep bodily caress deserves special mention: milk-duct massage. While surface stroking of a woman's breast excites her to some degree, the keenest sexual sensitivity centers in the milk ducts within and just behind the nipple. If her husband flips the nipple back and forth with the ball of his finger, the bending and straightening of the ducts stimulate nerve endings. Slightly more intense sensation stirs when he rolls the nipple underneath his thumb. Still stronger stimulation comes when he picks up the nipple between his thumb and index finger and rolls it back and forth. Some husbands prefer catching the nipple between their index and middle fingers, permitting sidewise rolling between the fingers, titillation with the thumb, thumb-rolling and a variety of exciting combinations which can bring a particularly sensitive woman to the very brink of orgasm.

In a few women, breast sensitivity is keenest in tissue buried an inch or more beneath the nipple. You can stimulate this area without bruising or damaging the breast by placing the flats of all four fingers below the nipple and stroking firmly (but not roughly) from above downward with the shaft of the thumb.

Embrace.

Embracing involves less variety than caress, but still contributes considerably to building up sexual excitement. Several points deserve your attention:

1. *Different initial embraces lead to extra variety in caress.*

If you start the serious build-up of sexual excitement locked in face-to-face embrace, your early caresses generally move from neck to shoulders to breast and back. With the wife's head in her husband's lap, her breasts, lower abdomen and thighs invite his prompt attention. A husband reaching from behind finds his hands holding his wife's breast or abdomen while his lips seek out her earlobes and neck. Although the embrace itself stirs little sexual feeling, the variety of caresses which different positions guarantee brings freshness to your sex life.

2. *Knocking and leg-climbing are proper to marital embrace.*

After a few weeks or months of marital satisfaction, you will find that bodily positions and motions similar to those occurring during intercourse become increasingly exciting. Simply pressing your abdomens together or lying with the husband locked between his lover's thighs will recall so many primitive delights that passion will run high. These maneuvers prove quite enticing without the risk that they may seem like teasing while pajamas or negligee still limit actual bodily contact. Some couples also enjoy close bodily contact during mouth, breast and general sex play. An intertwining of the legs to produce some friction of thigh on genitals sometimes adds excitement to breast and bodily caress.

3. *Contact between nude areas usually proves most enticing when quite gentle, at least until intercourse begins.*

If you disrobe completely before a sexual encounter or during early stages of intimate play, you will find that an embrace which barely brings soft breasts against strong chest, which lays the husband's thigh against his wife's buttock, or which brushes leg on leg proves much more enticing than a crushing hug. Gentle contact stirs the sexually sensitive light-touch nerves, while heavy pressure overwhelms them.

Naked embrace is simply a way of caressing with different body parts instead of with your hands. Like your hands, your other body parts stir excitement by moving lightly from place to place or shifting in rhythmic squeeze or stroke, not by pressing steadily against a sexually sensitive area. The female breast, the male genitals, the thighs and calves and feet can all produce light and enticing friction if properly applied.

Mouth-to-breast-and-body play.

Most couples wonder how far they can go in sex play without passing the bounds of normalcy. Let me reassure you on this point! Absolutely anything which does no physical injury and which does not replace intercourse as the means of resolving sexual excitement is perfectly normal. However, normalcy and wisdom need not always be identical, and most couples find it wise to set some limits on sex play other than those imposed by natural law. In caresses applied with the mouth to various body parts, these limits often take two different forms:

1. *Strong emotional taboos.*

While any form of caress which remains preliminary to intercourse is normal, many people whose inhibitions in no way interfere with their ability to form a sound sexual adjustment feel repelled or disturbed by mouth-to-genital and other forms of completely abandoned play. The emotional barrier involved must be more than simple neutrality. A woman who finds that caressing or kissing her husband's genitals in the final stages of precoital play helps to build his sexual excitement and increase both his satisfaction and his capacity to please her should certainly do so occasionally, even if she has no impulse or urge in that direction. But if the idea makes her feel positively repelled and she cannot force herself toward this act without intense emotional disturbance, then neither she nor her husband should insist upon this practice. Perhaps her attitude might change over the years, or perhaps the methods outlined in Chapter Five will

overcome her inhibitions, but you will find it best
not to force the issue so long as this revulsion exists.

2. *Sanitary limitations.*

The mouth normally contains many bacteria which
can cause infection to other body areas. The wife's
breast may fail to resist these germs during milk pro-
duction and for a short time thereafter. When a
woman is making milk for a new baby, her milk ducts
are filled with a perfect medium for bacterial growth.
An interval of mouth-breast sex play which would be
perfectly harmless at any other time can cause serious
infection during the nursing period. Even weeks after
the milk flow has ceased, blowing-type caresses may
drive enough saliva into the milk ducts to cause an
infection.

While many couples have no difficulty following
tonguing or other mouth-to-genital caresses of the
female organ, I have seen a number of women with
irritation and infection of the vagina which persisted
or recurred, despite use of usually effective medicines,
until the husband's mouth caresses were kept above
the waist. The indirect transmission of saliva to the
genitals causes irritation in many women, too, as by
use of saliva as a sexual lubricant or by finger transfer
to the genitals of mouth moisture left on the breast by
previous play.

While some couples ignore these sanitary hazards
without getting into any trouble, you can make your
play techniques entirely safe with only a few simple
rules. Omit mouth-to-breast play during the nursing
period, make it a general rule not to go back to
manual play *with the same breast* after mouth caresses,
and either omit mouth caresses of the wife's genitals

or eliminate them if any irritation or discharge
develops.

Acceptable techniques.

A great many varieties of mouth-to-breast and
mouth-to-body play fall well within the limits set
by sanitation and emotional constraint. Both sexes
respond to kisses and gentle nips of the neck, shoulders, chest or abdomen. Mouth play involving the
male genitals creates no sanitary problems, and has
some place in the sex life of certain couples. This
form of sex play is not perversion so long as it *precedes*
instead of *replaces* intercourse, but enough people
hold false beliefs in this regard that you should probably discuss the matter in advance and concede to any
major hesitancy. If neither of you feels any revulsion
or hesitation about this form of play, love nips along
the top of the erect penis or gentler kisses around its
head can bring sexual excitement to considerable
height.

A husband's mouth play with his wife's breasts gives
tremendous impetus to both parties' sexual excitement. Although a chain of kisses spiraling around the
breast sometimes proves a pleasant preliminary, most
mouth-breast play centers on the nipple area. At first,
very gentle frictions of the nipple against moist mouth
membranes excite the strongest response. Several techniques give this kind of contact:

¶ The husband holds the nipple button gently
between almost-limp lips, perhaps pouted
outward to bring only their moist, smooth
surfaces into contact. By rapid but gentle alter-

nate blowing and sucking, he makes the nipple move in and out between his stationary lips.

¶ With lips touching lightly or not at all, the husband laps at the nipple with his tongue, runs the tip of his tongue around and across the button, or tries to press the button back into the breast with the tip of his tongue and then move it rapidly from side to side.

¶ The husband takes the whole nipple area into his mouth. Tucking the tip of his tongue down behind his lower teeth, he pushes the body of his tongue forward underneath the nipple, presses it up so that it catches the nipple against the roof of the mouth, and slides it backward in a gentle milking motion. He repeats this action rhythmically.

Somewhat deeper pressure on the nipple stimulates the milk ducts beneath for added sexual arousal. Most couples find one or more of these methods satisfactory:

¶ The husband rolls his lips inward so that they cover his teeth and grasps the nipple button between them. By moving his jaw from side to side, he then rolls the nipple between firm surfaces.

¶ The husband takes the entire nipple into his mouth and milks it between the body of his tongue and his palate as above, but with some suction and firm pressure to make the stimulation deeper. Rocking the tongue from side to side adds interesting variety to this caress.

¶ As a final fillip at the end of an episode of mouth-breast play, the husband catches the nipple button gently between his lip-covered or bare teeth and either shakes his head gently or leans back to put the nipple under mild stretch.

Genital caresses.

When you become even mildly aroused sexually, stimulation of your genitals tends to excite your ardor further. After a few pleasant sexual experiences have followed close upon the handling or stimulation of your partner's genitals, the act of fondling intimate areas becomes linked with excitement, too. Both husband and wife can engage in this form of sex play in perfect confidence that it is normal and wholesome.

How to caress the female genitals.

If you are just starting your sex life together or if past wifely satisfaction has not yet led to full feminine sexual awakening, caresses of the clitoris will stir ardor much more effectively than deeper friction. Even after years of married life, you will probably want to keep most husbandly caresses at or near the feminine outlet. You can bring much more variety and actually increase the intensity of stimulation by specific genital caresses of the most responsive spots than by merely using one or two fingers to mimic intercourse.

Since the clitoris becomes erect and firm (just like the penis) during sexual excitement, you will find this organ easy to locate. The erect clitoris stands out in the aroused female like a firm rod imbedded in the soft surrounding tissues at the meeting of the two inner lips just in front of the vagina. There is no sense trying to locate this keenly sensitive organ beforehand, since it remains too soft and small to identify until ardor makes it swell.

When you start to caress the clitoris, the tissues in the area are usually more or less dry. Until they become moist with natural secretions or through lubrication, rubbing along the surface causes discomfort or irritation. Your earliest clitorine caresses must therefore remain free of surface friction. Two simple techniques qualify: the rolling-pin type caress, in which you roll your finger back and forth across either the tip or the base of the clitoris like a rolling pin, and the vibrating caress in which you jiggle the finger rapidly but with very small excursions so that the surface tissues can move *with* the finger within the range of their elasticity.

As more thorough sexual arousal brings the fluid-forming glands of the vagina into play, you can easily spread enough lubricating moisture over the clitoris to permit silky, non-irritating friction. However, you must usually transfer this moisture deliberately from the moist vulva and vagina to the vicinity of the clitoris, which itself has few lubricating glands. With a relatively inexperienced woman, you can best accomplish this purpose by simply repeatedly dipping the finger into the moist parts of the vagina and stroking the clitoris. The vaginal surface is usually moist quite close to the female outlet, so that you need not insert the finger more than half an inch or so. In this procedure, you are using the vagina as a source of fluid like an ink well, not as an object of sexual stimulation. The state of the clitoris and your manipulation of it deserve attention, with the vagina considered as a convenient pool of secretions rather than an object of caress.

With somewhat more sexual experience, most women develop sexual sensitivity in other areas besides the clitoris. Fluid-transferring caresses then become an important part of genital stimulation instead of mere adjuncts to clitorine stimulation. Stroking from behind forward along the inside of the large outer lips of the female organ or across the vaginal opening affords keen ardor-arousing stimulation while simultaneously moistening the clitoris for intercourse or direct caress. Soft, silky stroking rather than harsh rubbing works best. You will find many variations possible: one finger stroking up one side and then the other, tickling or vibrating titillation up one side and then the other, stroking along the sides of the vulva with one finger following each track, stroking from back to front with the flats of all four fingers joined (which you will find easiest if you hold your arm still and alternately open and close your hand in a snatching motion). If you must go up into the vagina to find enough fluid in the experienced woman, insert one or two fingers about half way in, press them fairly firmly against the front wall of the vagina so that you press this tissue and the underlying urinary tube between the pulps of your finger and the pelvic bone, then draw your fingers along the vaginal wall until you reach the clitoris. This caress usually lubricates the clitoris quite well while simultaneously imparting a considerable sexual thrill after thorough sexual awakening. Or you can use any of the vaginal caresses described below in alternation with clitorine stimulation to keep your fingers and the stimulated area moist.

A well lubricated clitoris responds keenly to friction either crosswise or lengthwise, at its tip or its base, back to front or front to back. You can stimulate the clitoris with the pulp of your finger, the side of your finger shaft, the back of your bent finger, or your thumb knuckle. While engaging in vaginal caress, you can occasionally rub the base of your index finger and its knuckle or the pulp of your thumb tip across or along the clitoris. Caresses can be slow or fast, steady or vibrating, rhythmic or irregular. Almost anything goes, with two exceptions: don't use the fingernail area because the delicate tissues in this area scratch very easily, and don't continue friction-type caresses after the clitoris begins to get dry without first transferring more lubricating fluid to it.

After full sexual awakening, several other parts of the female genitalia develop keen sexual sensitivity. A few weeks of marriage usually bring the inner lips into play. Like the clitoris, these folds of tissue require lubricating moisture before they will tolerate much rubbing. Their surface location makes even the gentlest caress keenly satisfying, however. You can stimulate the inner lips with simple one-finger stroking. You can pick up one lip between your thumb and finger, stroking along its length with light or moderate pressure or twanging it with picking motions. You can fold your index and middle fingers, then catch one inner lip between them for a sort of grinding or rolling caress which simultaneously presses one of the knuckles against the clitoris.

The inner lips contain erectile tissue like that found in the penis and clitoris, but their engorgement usually occurs only during the keenest sexual arousal. Thus inner-lip caresses not only give you a means of exciting your wife's ardor, but also a means of judging its extent. Although the degree to which the inner lips swell during full arousal varies from woman to

woman, you will usually find that during ideal arousal
the inner lips engorge so firmly that they protrude
and push the outer lips completely aside. The inner
lips simultaneously thicken into firm ridges instead of
delicate folds. This change is proof positive of your
wife's full passionate preparation. Although it may
occur only occasionally instead of in every encounter,
it gives you an excellent end-point toward which to
strive in precoital play.

The back corner of the vaginal outlet usually becomes sexually alive after a few months of marital
success. Since this area becomes moist quite early in
precoital play, you can both caress it simultaneously
and use it as a source of lubricating fluid for the
clitoris. Side to side friction along the back of the
vagina with the finger inserted half an inch to an inch
makes an excellent early genital caress. A rotary caress
in which you insert the finger an inch or so into the
outlet and move it rapidly in a circle also proves
exciting. When sexual excitement has been thoroughly
aroused just prior to intercourse, another special caress
sometimes gives quite a thrill. Pick up the muscle body
which lies just behind the vaginal opening with your
fingers part way in the vagina and your thumb tip on
the outside. Kneed these muscles between thumb and
fingers, jiggle them up and down or from side to side,
stretch them downward or alternately squeeze and
release them.

After six months or a year of reasonably satisfactory
connubial activity, most women develop rather keen
sexual sensitivity of the tube leading from the bladder
to the outside. This tube lies just in front of the
vagina, where it gets caught between the penis and the
pelvic bone. By running one or two fingers up along
the front wall of the vagina and pressing that wall

toward your wife's pubic bone, you can duplicate this stimulation. Rhythmic strokings, in-and-out vibration or kneading motions all give varied and intense effect. Unlike most genital caresses, which should be silky and light-touched, this one requires reasonably firm pressure to be effective.

Caresses of the vagina itself serve several useful purposes. You build sexual excitement through in-and-out motions of one or two fingers, through two-finger crawling motions or through twists of the wrist while the fingers are inserted and spread. You can judge the wife's preparedness through vaginal caress, and assure her comfort during intercourse by always waiting until the vagina is thoroughly moist and is sufficiently relaxed to admit two fingers with ease before making entry. Finally, intensive sex play either through the techniques discussed above or through finger motions simulating actual sex contact usually prove the easiest way to provide the necessary extra orgasms for women who need more than one climax in order to feel totally replete after intercourse or who need several more orgasms during each month than their husbands can otherwise provide. If you adopt this course, however, remember that after one orgasm the woman needs a few minutes of further play to regenerate her sexual excitement before she is ready for the final, intercourse-generated climax.

How to caress the male genitals.

Proper caresses of the male genitals do nothing to speed the male climax, and in fact often have the opposite action. By building male excitement to a high level before the first contact of intercourse, you make that contact seem almost quieting, and keep the sexual stimulations of the first insertion from causing a quick climax. Moreover, you prolong considerably the period of preliminary sex play, which generally makes full feminine fruition more likely. You avoid both the hair-trigger urgency which most men develop if they hold off until their excitement is on the wane and the poor quality of erection which makes an inadequately stimulated male an uninspiring sex partner.

Gentle, early genital caresses usually center upon the scrotum and the top surface of the penile shaft. Light stroking of the back of the scrotum, starting perhaps an inch or two behind the sac itself and running either down or around the dangling appendage, often proves effective. If you let the scrotum and its contents lie free upon the flats of your four fingers, several varieties of caress become easy. You can bobble the testes about with your fingers, gently scratch the back of the scrotum with your fingernails or the front of it with your thumb, or roll folds of the scrotal skin (avoiding the testicles) between thumb and fingers. Pinching caresses of the scrotal area can also be quite exciting if reserved for the final phases of sex play.

A quivering caress with the fingers patting lightly along the top of the penis, flicking of this area with the index finger, and scratching or pinching it all produce keen masculine excitement. Stroking along the top of the penis from its base to its tip generally spurs male ardor without precipitating a quick climax. Grasping or clutching the penis without any up-and-down friction also stirs excitement without upsetting harmonious sex pacing. As a final fillip before sexual intercourse, some women occasionally administer a "snake-bite" caress just beneath the head of the penis, grasping the shaft in one hand and the head in the other, then quickly twisting the two hands in opposite directions in a sort of wringing motion. By going one way then the other with each hand for two or three quick jolts, you can bring any erection to a perfect peak.

Like the female urinary tube, the male one quickly develops keen sexual sensitivity. Caresses where this tube runs along the bottom surface of the penis must generally be limited to tickling, scratching or pinching, which stimulate the skin instead of the underlying urinary tube. Deeper frictions might bring on a male climax and end the prospect of intercourse for you both. However, you can stimulate the male urinary tube before it reaches the penis without this danger. This tube runs close to the skin surface for an inch or two behind the scrotum. By pushing the tips of one or two fingers hard up into this area and waggling them to and fro, you can give your husband an added sexual thrill.

The final trigger of male sexual excitement is the frenulum, the thin fold of tissue just beneath the penile head. This fold and the small area of tissue adjoining are a man's keenest sexual triggers. In the early stage of sex play, you had best leave this area strictly alone. Caresses here will bring the male to a pitch of excitement demanding intercourse in a few moments. When you feel fairly well along in your own excitement, you might titillate or tickle this spot very briefly, just enough to make your partner catch his breath and come at you with increased vigor. A quick but gentle scratch across this area with your fingernail will bring a further thrill, and is perfectly safe once you feel fully prepared for any sexual assault which it inspires. You can almost always trigger intercourse when you have reached the point of distinct yearning for it simply by pinching this nerve center once or twice or using the snake-bite caress described above with your hands meeting at this area.

How to put this chapter's advice to work for you.

If you are beginners.

Remember: the wife always goes along with her husband's urges, the couple strives for wifely comfort and masculine control, and neither need expect much satisfaction at first.

Take plenty of time in mouth-to-mouth play and simple bodily caress. By thoroughly arousing mutual excitement in this way, any barriers of modesty which otherwise would limit your sex play will fall.

Both partners should use their hands in embraces and caress constantly.

When the husband starts mouth-to-breast play, the wife should caress his earlobes, his neck, his shoulders and his back. As her passion becomes intense, she should press her vibrating fingertips into his back and otherwise incite his further excitement. Murmurs of appreciation and loving remarks help him to judge which attentions please the most. In early mouth-breast play, the husband should use air pressures to push the nipple in and out between his moist lips, titillate the nipple with his tongue, and perhaps draw it into his mouth for gentle rolling against the roof of his mouth. He should generally start genital caresses before bringing the milk-duct nerve centers into play.

In early months of marriage, the husband should forget all other parts of the genitals except the clitoris. At first, he should roll the tip or base beneath his finger with a rocking, rolling-pin caress involving no surface friction. His wife should respond with ardent caresses, remembering that fingering the clitoris does little to maintain his excitement. She should express any delight she feels freely with words or other utterances, and should deepen and intensify her own caresses. As her sex organs begin to flow with moisture, the husband should alternately insert the tip of his finger and rub across or along the clitoris several times. After he has spread lubricating fluid over the area, he can put a bit of friction into his clitorine caress. At this stage, deeper breast play with the fingers (on the other breast) or with the mouth seems quite apt. Rolling the nipple between lip-covered teeth or working it between the body of the tongue and the roof of the mouth bring most women great delight. The woman can prolong this play phase best by maintaining or increasing her husband's excitement with deeper and more intensive caresses. Genital caresses along the top of the penile shaft or tickling, scratching, stroking and bobbling of the scrotal area work quite well. Finally, the wife can signal her desire for an end to dalliance with a pinch, a snake-bite or a clutching caress of the penis or the frenulum if she so desires. Such methods seem indelicate in bald words, but in actual execution seem no more than passionate response. On one point all wives generally agree: a husband does better by them when they *force* him to start intercourse by intensely exciting caress than if they *ask* him or *tell* him to get on with things when he has not yet expressed that intent. No husband has to wait for his wife's final triggering of his sex desire. He can get on with sex whenever his own urges or his wife's palpable arousal so demand. But the wise wife

always triggers her husband's urge if she can't stand
to wait, instead of taking the obvious initiative.

If you are old-timers.

The big problem with your preliminaries is generally that they have become curt and almost routine.
If anything, you need to spend *more* time and effort
—certainly not less—stirring each other's excitement
as the years go by. Use this chapter's suggestions to
add new variety and intensity to your sex play.

Wives who find themselves indulging in loving
service despite a lack of ardor should play an active
role in preliminary sex play instead of merely ac-
quiescing. Sex play is an essential part of the build-up
of excitement through which you give your husband
satisfaction. When you play the feminine role specifically for the purpose of bringing satisfaction, adequate
sex play helps tremendously in achieving that goal.
The habit of taking an active part even when you feel
poorly disposed toward sex often leads to delayed but
genuinely passionate response. It definitely contributes
to later development of ardor in many women. Every
episode in which you actively extend yourself in totally
willing service to someone you love builds feminine
passion by pleasant emotional involvement in sex.
When such involvement has attached intense values
to sex play and intercourse, ardent response and
orgasm often result.

When you get to genital caress, you will find the
clitoris almost unimportant after a few years of
sexual experience. The husband's first caresses should
spread moisture along the outer lips and to the clitoris,
with gentle one- or two-finger stroking either from

back to front or along the vagina's front wall. Snatch-like, four-finger caresses work quite well at the next stage, perhaps alternating with thumb-knuckle caresses of the clitoris. The inner lips deserve everything husbands give them in the way of stroking, grinding and titillation. If your wife has prominent inner lips, you will find their erection a guide to impending super-passionate embrace.

If you have found from experience that feminine fervor takes more than one orgasm for its control, or if you cannot get together often enough to completely control feminine desire, bring about one feminine orgasm through intensive love-play. Always delay intercourse for several minutes thereafter to revive female excitement. You will find such prolonged play is always possible if the wife says: "Let me keep you going" instead of just "Give me more." Her job in caressing and kissing and otherwise keeping up her husband's excitement is just as important as his in stimulating her own orgasm. Without his wife's attentions, no husband can prolong sex play very long without losing erection. Remember, *couple* effort for *couple* satisfaction! That's the key to well-paced, harmonious sex play.

4.
The Third Key to
Soundly Satisfying Sex:
Varied Sex Positions

Most couples try a dozen different sex positions in their first year, settle on two or three for the next five years, and thereafter find themselves using one particular position almost all the time.

Precisely the opposite course makes a great deal more sense. In the early days of marriage, sexual sensitivity in the wife still centers sharply on the clitoris, so that the stimulation offered to other areas by varied sex positions means little or nothing to her. Her newness to marriage and the fact that childbirth has not stretched her tissues make a snug fit inevitable in straight-away positions and simultaneously create real risk of pain from too great penetration or from positions bringing the penis into play at a great angle. The novelty of sex itself has not worn off, so that different approaches to it are scarcely necessary to inspire interest.

A few years later, the whole picture has changed. Wives thrill to stimulation in new areas and never suffer painful stretching from deep penetration or unusual angles of approach. Husbands find that some positions restore pleasant snugness to connubial union, and that variety in position quickly eliminates any yearning for new bedfellows. Moreover, the sexual skills required for masterful conduct of relations in many different positions come only with experience and effort. A newly-married couple really needs months to consummate in fullest harmony even if they stick to the three basic positions. Having passed this apprentice phase, most couples can achieve new heights of intimate delight by applying themselves in ways which would lead only to disharmony and failure right at first.

Position and other helps in dealing with virginity.

Preparation for the honeymoon should always include two frequently omitted steps:

First, the prospective wife should have a medical examination with special attention to the virginal membrane, preferably at least six weeks before marriage. If that membrane still remains intact (which it may not, even in the most virtuous) and especially if tightness has prevented use of internal tampons for feminine hygiene, she should probably ask her doctor to dispose of it.

To avoid any possible misunderstanding later, perhaps she should discuss this situation with her fiancé beforehand. However, both husband and wife will ultimately profit from a painless and pleasant initial sexual experience. They would be very foolish indeed to impose or accept a burden of sexual suffering merely to support an outmoded tradition. Your doctor can deal painlessly with the membrane in a matter of minutes if it might otherwise cause you a painful initiation into sex.

Second, whether or not the virginal membrane has

been dealt with by a doctor, the prospective bride should stretch the opening to the vagina for a head start on marital adjustment. Instead of ordinary lubrication, she should generally apply a moderately thick layer of Surfacaine ointment to the area and wait three to five minutes for the deadening action of that ointment to take effect. She should then lubricate one finger (preferably one with a short, well-filed fingernail) with more ointment and insert it slowly into the vagina. If long fingernails create a risk of injury or if modesty prevents direct finger contact, a rubber stall can be used. Usually one to five minutes every day devoted to widening the vaginal opening results in proper stretching and relaxation in four to six weeks. When one finger can be inserted all the way to its base, gentle stretching of the vagina forward and backward and from side to side helps. Try insertion of two fingers as soon as there is plenty of room for one. When the vagina accommodates two fingers all the way to their base without discomfort, properly conducted sexual intercourse usually proves entirely comfortable.

When the wedding night arrives, Surfacaine ointment still has advantages over ordinary lubricants. Remember that your objectives in the first few sexual encounters are *feminine comfort and masculine control*. A slight deadening of sensation aids you in both of these goals at only slight sacrifice in sexual satisfaction. If the husband finds that he cannot freely insert two fingers to their bases when sex play has reached its climax, he should probably avoid sexual contact even if his wife cries for it. Once his sex organ presses against moist female membranes, biological pressures become almost unbearable. A few nights of intensive sex play before he puts himself in this position will generally assure a smoother beginning for the couple's sex life if a tight opening makes comfortable union unlikely. As soon as two fingers pass easily into the female cavern, sexual entrance can usually be accomplished with ease.

Unless the hymen has been cut by a physician, it will continue to partially obstruct the female opening even after the latter has been stretched by self-manipulation or sex play. The main portion of this membrane usually lies like a crescent-shaped veil across the back of the vaginal opening: Its position is such that it moves farther up over the vaginal opening when the legs are brought forward than when they are down flat or even bent backward somewhat. If you have difficulty accomplishing initial entrance, a special position may prove helpful in getting past the hymen. The bride lies on her back with two pillows under her hips and with her legs down as flat as possible to carry the hymen back out of the way. Her husband approaches from directly above, so that the penis occupies almost a vertical position at first contact. He places the tip of the penis (which should be well lubricated) against the very front corner of the female opening and slides it along in close contact with the upper surface thereof. This approach will usually allow the penis to slip past the hymen with reasonable ease. The wife can then cautiously bring her knees up as far as the stretching hymen will permit. The membrane sometimes tears during this change in posture. If it does not, you should make a further attempt to rupture it before commencing sexual motions. A combination burlesque bump by the woman and straight down pressure with the penile shaft will almost always cause a clear tear without unduly painful pulling if the membrane is reasonably thin.

Rupture of the virginal membrane generally causes slight bleeding, which may continue for five or ten minutes or even longer. If this bleeding persists after sexual relations are complete, lie on your back with your legs together for a few minutes. If bleeding still persists, place a small ball of absorbent cotton or a few pieces of shredded facial tissues between the outer lips and in contact with the bleeding area, then resume the legs-together position. Leave the fiber in place for twelve hours, then soak it loose with a tub bath to avoid new bleeding. Blood loss from a torn hymen is very rarely dangerous and usually stops without difficulty. In the occasional case where it persists for more than a few hours, a doctor can readily stop it for you.

As soon as rupture of the virginal membrane permits relatively unimpeded sexual contact, you can shift into a more comfortable sex position.

The basic lying-on-your-sides position.

The best initial position in commencing or revamping your sex life is one which places both of you comfortably lying on your sides. You can get into this position most easily by making sexual contact with the wife on her back. She spreads and bends her legs. Her husband supports his body above her on his hands and knees. He brings his penis into contact with the vagina (but not necessarily into deep penetration). The wife then brings her legs up until they rest against her husband's flanks, and the couple rolls together onto one side or the other, remaining face to face.

This position has several advantages during the early phase of couple adaptation. The husband can pause for as long as necessary to control biological pressures without either tiring himself by supporting his weight or crushing his wife by failing to do so. The male's angle of approach lines up the penis almost perfectly with the vagina, keeping the amount of stretching of that organ to a minimum (which is vital during the honeymoon). Both partners have their hands free for caresses. The breast areas, the buttocks, the back and the thighs are readily available for such attentions, which are especially necessary to maintain excitement when too rapid progress toward a male climax calls for suspension of sexual frictions, as often happens during early experiences. And the relatively limited range of movement available to both parties (especially the wife) keeps even quite poorly synchro-nized efforts from leading to loss of engagement or to painful over-stretching of genital tissues.

Whether you have had previous sexual experience or not you should probably stick to this first position almost exclusively until you have learned to control the biologic pressures on the male quite thoroughly. Such control is your main couple aim (aside from feminine comfort) during the early weeks. The wife should maintain her husband's excitement with words, kisses, caresses, and such sexual motions as she can manage unless he signals her to be still. The husband should cautiously try various sexual motions and rhythms with long pauses in between to restore his sexual composure. These cautious and interrupted excursions work best in an on-the-sides position, at least until the final surge of the climax (for which you can roll into a wife-on-her-back posture if you wish).

In these early episodes, the wife will almost always lose much or all of her sexual excitement during the long pauses and cautious movements. She will almost never reach an orgastic climax.

However, such sessions make a tremendous difference to later couple harmony in several ways. If both of you can learn how to judge and influence the husband's biological state, you can prolong sexual activity quite considerably if you wish. A wife who thinks about what she can contribute to her husband's satisfaction for a few sessions when she is not overwhelmed with passion discovers a dozen tricks and caresses which she can later apply, to both her husband's and her own delight, when passion holds her in its grip. The husband rids himself of accumulated biological tensions which might otherwise make his climaxes premature. And both parties gain sexual confidence from totally controlled experiences. The husband feels entirely secure in his sexual capacity when he can say: "There, I've mastered myself so completely that I can go until I *decide* to end it." The wife feels perfect confidence in both her attractions and skills when she can say: "There, I've proved that I can satisfy him one hundred per cent without crowding the pace."

After you have learned sexual control, you can start to work toward a mutual climax on suitable occasions. Now that you know what you have to do to keep the husband going, try to bring feminine excitement to a high pitch before commencing intercourse. Some men can go right into a wife-stimulating sexual rhythm without any initial pause, especially when they have had plenty of sexual relief recently. Others must rebuild feminine ardor which has sagged during the initial pause. In either case, you can frequently win your first sexual success by a simple shift in your attention from merely achieving male control to using that control to make the climax coincide with a peak of feminine excitement. The on-your-sides posture generally provides all you need in the way of stimulation.

The wife-astride postures.

You will probably find several real advantages in the sex positions which place the woman on top, both for improving couple cooperation in sex and for giving new thrills and variation. Probably you should master control of the male biological pressures in the basic lying-on-your-side position first: the wife-astride postures give the woman such freedom of movement that she can easily push her husband into an early climax unless she is thoroughly familiar with the exact limits to which she can go without over-stimulating him and has achieved sufficient self-control to freeze in immobile rest whenever he signals for a pause. Newlyweds need to delay the astride postures for several weeks and to try them with some caution, because the very deep penetration involved sometimes stretches the unaccustomed vagina painfully during the more violent movements. However, as soon as you have achieved fundamental couple control and a degree of vaginal relaxation, the wife-astride postures offer these advantages:

1. *The husband can caress the clitoris freely during intercourse, as well as the breasts, buttocks, thighs and abdomen.*

During sexual episodes early in marriage when diffuse bodily stimulation and stimulation of the clitoris mean more to the woman than other genital frictions, the husband can keep one finger or a thumb constantly on the clitoris and the other hand busy with various intimacies for as long as his wife desires. Such stimulation builds the emotional linkage of genital friction with sexual excitement, and actually speeds the full awakening of a woman's sexual nature.

2. *By letting the wife set her own pace and govern the intensity of her genital stimulation, both partners can learn what speed and pressures suit her best.*

When you have learned what couple measures will keep a quick male climax from spoiling your delights, your next step toward sexual success as a couple is to learn what stimulations will bring about full feminine satisfaction. The new bride doesn't know exactly what will suit her, but the wife-astride postures let her experiment until she finds out. The experienced woman knows exactly what she wants, and not only gets it through this posture but also shows her husband what she would like him to do.

3. *A few episodes in a position demanding feminine initiative often conquer false modesty and sexual hesitation.*

Both the active and the passive partner to each caress or maneuver benefit in every sexual episode. However, many couples only explore half of the available maneuvers, since the wives suppress their carnal impulses in misguided modesty. When the wife takes over the reins of intercourse for a few impassioned episodes, her whole sexual behavior often sheds these false constraints, and she comes into her own as an actively passionate partner to mutually intensified sex play and union.

4. *Several motions possible in astride postures speed the woman toward her climax without greatly affecting the man.*

So long as the woman keeps her genitals pressed down upon her husband's body, his organ receives no in-and-out friction at all. If she slides down along his body until the top of his penis presses firmly against her clitoris, she can get intensive stimulation without in any way speeding him toward a climax. Writhing side-to-side movement, rocking motions, and rotary hip-twirling achieve this end splendidly. If the woman sticks mainly to these movements and lets her husband simultaneously move in and out as much as he wishes, she can receive very intense stimulation without bringing matters to an early end.

Although all three main astride postures share these big advantages, each has separate good and bad points of its own.

Most couples fall first into the *astride position in which the man lies on his back with his wife's legs beside his flanks.* Sex play should thoroughly arouse the lady's ardor beforehand, since the deep penetration involved in this position may cause pain unless the woman's vagina is thoroughly lubricated and relaxed. Usually, you commence intercourse with the wife on her back, then roll over until she is on top. She half sits on her husband's genitals and half kneels on the bed beside him to gain purchase for easier movement. In this position, she can lean back to make heavy sexual friction by misaligning the penis and vagina or lean forward and slide the contact area back to bring her clitoris firmly against the penile shaft. She can move from side to side, rock back and forth or twirl in a level circular motion which combines with her husband's thrust to produce a unique barber-pole effect.

A few women find that the weight of the internal organs presses an ovary or some other tender structure down where the deeply penetrating penis can catch it, with resulting twinges of pain during intercourse.

These women must either move with some caution or adopt one of the other astride positions. However, most women find that once the vagina has been stretched by a few months of marriage or by childbirth they can move with absolute abandon to produce every type of sexual stimulation which they enjoy or require in the standard astride posture.

Both early and late in marriage, a somewhat different astride position has considerable advantages. In this variation, the husband *spreads his legs apart and the wife keeps her knees between his thighs* (although she must usually keep her knees a few inches apart to leave room for genital contact). She can support part of her weight upon her elbows if she wishes, although her husband usually will not object if she lets her body fall against his. A pillow under the husband's hips may facilitate genital contact in some cases.

This position brings the penis very firmly against the clitoris, which makes it very satisfying for women still in the course of sexual awakening. It involves less depth of penetration than the previously described astride posture, and does not press possibly tender structures down within reach of penile battering. Thus newlyweds can often enjoy this posture sooner than the standard astride position, and the woman who sometimes suffers spasms of pain when sitting erect upon her husband's genitals can almost always indulge comfortably while lying flat upon his whole body. Furthermore, a woman whose capacity to satisfy her husband has diminished due to the vaginal stretching of several childbirths can often restore snugness of fit in this position simply by moving her thighs closer together.

The third variety of astride position works best

with *the husband slumped down slightly on an ordinary straight chair*. His wife sits on his lap facing him, with one leg on either side of his body. Most couples assume this position well in advance of actual intercourse, often conducting most of their sex play in it. Both partners have their hands entirely free and can caress almost all of the sexually sensitive areas in a dozen different ways. The position also permits a unique form of sex contact in which the head of the penis lies within the vaginal opening with the woman sitting just far enough back so that it can rub but cannot penetrate. Her husband can bounce her on his lap or make typical sexual motions while she remains free to rock and slide or writhe from side to side, all in conjunction with caresses of the breasts, buttocks, thighs, and such genital areas as are not in contact. The wife can move from this preliminary position into complete sexual contact simply by sliding forward a few inches, or can settle into an intermediate position where she can rock forward for full sex contact or rock backward for further play. By mixing these two in just the right proportions to maintain the husband's excitement without precipitating his climax, they can keep up keen and mutual stimulation for much longer than in most other sex positions and achieve very gratifying communion indeed.

The fundamental wife-lies-on-her-back position.

Although you will usually find it easier to achieve your first complete sexual success by using an on-the-side or astride position, the fundamental wife-lies-on-her-back position allows somewhat more intense conjoint sexual activity. In this position, the wife lies on her back with her legs spread, her knees partly bent and her heels either digging into the mattress or cupped in the hollows at the back of her husband's knees. The husband gets up on his hands and knees directly above her body, with his knees together between her legs. After sexual entrance, he may shift part of his weight to his elbows so that his hands are partially free, or he may curl his back to allow some mouth-to-breast play. However, in this position the male must usually depend mainly on sexual motions to stimulate his partner. The wife, on the other hand, has both hands completely free and can easily reach most of her husband's sexually sensitive parts. She has good purchase with her legs to permit to-and-fro and rotary motions (as discussed in the next chapter). She can take quite an active part in intercourse.

The fundamental wife-on-her-back position calls for somewhat more skill and control than the side posture. The husband usually finds that he cannot relax readily to control rapid progress toward a climax. In fact, the strained position in which he must hold himself makes some quivering and muscular tension inevitable even if he stops all sexual activity. The fact that the wife's sexual activity in this position can easily kick her husband into climax, which is not generally true in the side positions, adds to the control problem. Thus both husband and wife must keep the man's sexual excitement somewhat below the level which precipitates a climax, and both must expect an occasional quick conclusion while they are learning the necessary fine control.

However, the main reason for mastering couple control in a simpler framework before you undertake the standard posture is that this position calls for synchronized sexual movement, which requires considerable concentration and often proves too distracting until you have thoroughly mastered all other basic skills. At first, the wife will find it easiest to synchronize her actions by keeping one or both hands lightly on her husband's hip or buttock, being careful not to take the pace-setting role away from him by leading, but simply timing her own movements to correspond. The husband should generally limit his motions both in frequency and in extent to allow his wife to follow them in perfect rhythm, especially when one or both begin to approach the climax. At this point, instinct will push you toward such rapid action that synchronized movement will break down unless you use deliberate restraint. The satisfaction you will receive through matched harmony (discussed at length in the next chapter) will well repay the extra self-control, though.

Approaches from the rear.

Until several weeks of sexual activity have thoroughly stretched the vagina, you usually can choose only one other approach with certainty of wifely comfort: that in which the husband approaches from behind rather than from in front of his wife. The easiest position for this approach finds both partners lying on their sides.

The lying-on-sides posture with approach from the rear.

In this position, the wife lies on her side with her knees drawn partially up. Her husband lies on the same side just behind her, with his chest fairly far away from her back in order to bring the angle of the penis and the vagina into alignment.

This position gives little chance of achieving an orgasm for the wife during the early months of marriage, since it permits little sexual stimulation of the clitoris. Later in the course of sexual adjustment, the wife usually gets moderate sexual satisfaction in this posture. The husband can derive considerable satisfaction at any stage, although the fact that his wife can contribute virtually nothing in the way of either movement or caress limits his horizons somewhat.

When either fatigue or illness makes the wife prefer a highly passive and inactive role, she can let her husband satisfy himself through an approach from the rear while she lies on her side. Throughout the years of marriage, a number of such occasions will arise. The moderate satisfaction available in this way will usually keep the husband happy, the variety in sex posture may contribute something to your sex life as a couple, and the almost totally inactive female role will throw no strain upon the wife. When you undertake intercourse on these terms, however, you will probably need some artificial lubrication. Glycerine-base lubricating jellies (such as K-Y Jelly) should be used if you use any rubber products for conception control, and either petroleum jelly (Vaseline) or glycerine-base jellies if you do not.

Approach from the rear also may prove well suited to your first encounter after a separation. This position permits a great deal of fondling and extra stimulation during intercourse. The husband has both hands free and can use them on breasts, thighs, abdomen, buttocks and even on the clitoris. He can make barely enough sex motions to keep his erection firm and incite his wife with keen sex play to the very verge of a climax before he cuts loose. Even if his staying power is cut to a few fast strokes by long continence, he may be able to satisfy his wife to some extent in this way.

A few women make their sexual adjustment poorly because of a high-placed clitoris. If you find it easy to elicit a feminine orgasm by sex play or by genital caress at the conclusion of intercourse, but almost impossible to do so during intercourse itself, a high clitoris is usually at fault. Check on the situation with one finger during normal sexual relations. Unless you can rub the shaft of the penis against the clitoris in normal postures, you will have to depend heavily on clitorine caresses during intercourse until sexual awakening makes other genital areas more sensitive. Approach from the rear and the astride postures allow caressing of the clitoris during intercourse more easily than other postures, and thus facilitate this process.

Other approaches from the rear.

You can also use the basic approach from the rear in several other postures. The wife can get up on her hands and knees, then lower her chest to the bed (usually with a pillow underneath to promote comfort) while the husband kneels behind her. This position occasionally leads to pregnancy in women who have otherwise been unable to conceive, because any tendency toward a displaced uterus is corrected by the pull of gravity on the inner organs and because the discharged semen tends to pool right at the mouth of the womb. It permits somewhat more vigorous sexual motions than the same approach while lying on your sides, and also involves some extra friction due to an angulated alignment of penis and vagina. During intercourse and at the climax, stroking, kneading and clutching caresses of the wife's thighs, buttocks and back add pleasing excitement. These unusual genital and bodily stimulations make the wife-kneeling approach a pleasant variant. However, male motion must be almost continuous and the woman's position is quite fatiguing so that most couples make intercourse in this position rather quick. Both the position itself and the noises which frequently result from a tendency of the vagina to suck air when inverted make absolute privacy necessary. These limitations keep most couples from using this position very frequently unless they are trying to promote fertility with it.

If you have such a rapid sex pace that you need a lot of variations to keep from wearying of each other, you can also try the approach-from-the-rear with both partners standing or with the husband standing while the wife kneels at the edge of the bed. The wife's automatic muscle-quivers in these somewhat strained positions lend a new sensation to both partners, but this sensation is not so appealing that most couples come back frequently for more.

The angulated alignment postures.

After childbirth or several months of marriage have stretched the vagina somewhat, postures in which the penis enters at an angle different from that natural to the female genital tube become practical and pleasant.

After a year or so of marriage, most couples find that new sensitivities along the front wall of the vagina make sexual intercourse very pleasing to the wife when the angle of entrance forces the tip of the penis against this area. After sexual entrance in the usual wife-on-her-back posture, the husband raises his chest as high as possible without losing genital contact. The wife lifts her legs high. The man then supports his weight on one hand and passes the other arm across the woman's leg so that her heel rests on his shoulder. He repeats this action on the other side. Once the wife's heels are hooked on her husband's shoulders, both partners can relax most of their weight-supporting effort, since the natural recoil of the legs almost balances the man's weight. The wife can make virtually no sexual motions in this posture and is somewhat limited in which of her husband's body parts she can reach, so that her only contribution to male excitement must usually be through murmurs and cries of appreciation. The male makes up for his mate's immobility with vigorous and sustained action. He probably should only undertake this position when he is thoroughly rested and in good health. The resulting keen and different feminine delight makes this position definitely deserve a place in every couple's life, though.

A few women find that hooking their heels on their husband's shoulders places their thigh muscles under some strain or proves uncomfortable in some other way. A compromise posture brings the tip of the penis against the front vaginal wall without these strains. Simply place two pillows under the lady's hips before commencing intercourse, and let her draw her knees up close to her chest after sexual entry. This position gives somewhat weaker stimulation of the nerves which the heels-on-shoulders posture titillates so exquisitely, but allows more opportunity for the wife to caress and fondle her mate during intercourse.

Most couples find another position with angulated alignment useful on a few occasions when fatigue or illness requires sexual relief with a minimum of exertion or during an advanced pregnancy. This is the

crossed position, in which the wife lies on her back
with her legs partly folded and the husband lies on
his side with the axis of his body crosswise to hers, as
if he is a bench upon which she is sitting, with the
penis inserted from behind her thighs instead of between them. The man can add somewhat to his wife's
pleasure by massaging the clitoris during intercourse
in this position. The woman can make no sexual motions to speak of with her body, but can sometimes
boost her husband's climax with a few abdominal
pinches or clutching caresses of his thighs. The intensity of sexual pleasure in this position falls somewhat short of that in most other postures no matter
how you supplement it. However, you may find this
approach quite useful when more vigorous ones would
be a strain.

Lastly, you can snug up the fit of a very relaxed
vagina if the bearing of several children has made for
excess laxity by using a position in which the husband
straddles his wife instead of approaching from between
her thighs. An extra pillow or two under the woman's
hips helps to bring her genitals up for easy access. She
must generally separate her legs somewhat and bend
her knees part way, both in order to prevent painful
pressure where the penis passes under the front pelvic
bone and in order to gain purchase for sexual movement. However, she can substantially tighten the grip
her organ makes upon the penis by bringing her
thighs closer together after the man's entrance and by
straightening her legs as far as comfort permits. Relatively short sexual strokes with both partners in
synchronized or syncopated rhythm usually gives the
most intensive stimulation in this position. During
pauses and lulls, the husband usually finds consider-

able opportunity for mouth-breast play, since his wife is stretched full length and his own back is sharply bowed.

How and when to use the various sex positions.

Both honeymooners and old hands who want to rehabilitate or enliven their sex lives should probably stick with the basic lying-on-your-sides posture for several sessions. Deal first with the virginal membrane; if your doctor did not eliminate that problem for you, always assure feminine comfort with adequate pre-coital play and use of lubricants or Surfacaine ointment if necessary. Your next goal should be deliberate couple control of the male climax. The lying-on-your-sides position offers considerable advantages in this pursuit. You can also develop the habit of continual caress in the on-your-sides postures, since both of you have your hands free and every area from ear lobes to buttocks and from upper back to scrotum lie readily in reach. Kisses, love nips, breast play and squeals or murmurs of appreciation and endearment also help to maintain sexual excitement while you master the basic sex art.

After you can control male progress fairly well, you can usually manage your first completely mutual sexual success. A vigorous, instinct-governed climax in the wife-lies-on-her-back position usually wraps up this episode, but you can always wait until the last minute to shift into this position. Male control is still the essence of sexual success at this stage, and the wife is seldom ready to make much use of her freedom to move in harmony with her husband without ruining couple control. The wife-astride postures deserve early trial,

as soon as sexual activity has stretched the vagina
enough to make deep penetration comfortable. Newlyweds should usually stick to the astride position in
which the wife's legs lie between her husband's, both
because this posture usually prevents over-penetration
and because it brings the clitoris into closer contact
with the penis. Long-married couples can use the
standard wife-erect or the chair-borne astride posture.
In any case, the husband can usually keep one finger
busy at the clitoris throughout the early stages of
intercourse and add very active breast or buttock
stimulation with the other hand. The wife should
avoid bouncing movements until she is on the verge
of orgasm, since motions which involve in-and-out
movement of the penis often speed her husband's
climax. She should talk freely of her enjoyments,
though, remembering that these early episodes help as
much by improving couple awareness of each other's
likes and dislikes as by favorable individual experiences.

After you have mastered male control in the lying-
on-your-sides posture and explored female response to
various stimulations and rhythms in one of the astride
postures, you can try the more difficult synchronized
movements of the wife-on-her-back posture. Most
wives find that they can most easily develop the responsive rhythm necessary in this posture (and discussed at length in the next chapter) when they are
concentrating on husband-pleasing effort than when
they are entirely in the grips of passion. The wife
should usually signal for change into this posture
from either the on-your-sides or the astride one, perhaps with some remark which lets her husband know
her situation, like "Let's see whether I can give you
an extra good time tonight."

After rolling into position, she should at first keep one hand always on her husband's buttock to guide her in his rhythm, using the other hand to caress his abdomen, flanks or back. Both partners should strive for an even rhythm straight through to the climax in this position, even if the slow beat required by their inexperience proves less than fully satisfying. You will soon develop enough skill to achieve keen masculine satisfaction in this posture. After six or eight episodes, you will find that responsive feminine movements are almost automatic. Concentration on deliberately-timed movements no longer proves distracting to the wife. Intercourse in this position becomes equally gratifying for both partners, and practical on occasions of intensely mutual passion as well as when loving fulfillment of her feminine role is the woman's main goal.

Other sex positions have special uses, and may also help to keep your interest in each other alive by adding variety. Approach from the rear while lying on your sides and the crossed position will help tide you over periods of illness, fatigue, or advanced pregnancy. Wife's-legs-raised postures give special feminine thrills after full sexual awakening, several months to a year after successful marital adjustment. You should not adopt legs-up positions as standard because they allow too little feminine movement and too little variation in caress to keep your sex life fresh and interesting, but every woman deserves the ecstatic thrills of these positions at least a few times in each year. A woman with a birth-stretched vagina can please her husband best if he straddles her so that she can draw her thighs together to snug up the fit. A bride whose clitoris lies too high for friction against the penis deserves thorough finger massage during intercourse in the astride and approach from the rear postures until her sexual sensitivities spread. Finally, you may find that intercourse with the wife in knee-chest posture improves couple fertility if you have difficulty achieving pregnancy.

5.
The Fourth Key to
Soundly Satisfying Sex:
A Controlled
Sexual Crescendo

You do not need to abandon yourself to instinct in order to gain repletion, any more than you have to bolt your food to assuage ordinary hunger. In fact, you gain more repletion at the end if you take plenty of time with sex. Sex-generated tranquility spreads slowly to every pore of both your bodies during the mid-phase of intercourse, and seems to explode in every area it has reached at orgasm. A quick climax is like a grenade going off in your genitals sending bits of contentment into every limb, but a climax reached after full sexual transportation is more like a planned demolition with dynamite strapped to every body part.

Fundamental couple control.

The few moments after you establish genital contact have more than any other to do with your chances of achieving total and mutual sexual success. If instinct gets free rein over your movements, it brings the husband to his conclusion in a matter of seconds. He gets only fast animal relief, and his wife gets such brief stimulation that she gets satisfaction only if she has been played to the brink of orgasm beforehand.

Avoiding a fast male climax is like keeping yourselves from being swept over a waterfall. If you let the natural course of events carry you along until you are at the brink of disaster, the most extreme attempts to stop or to back water win only a brief delay. A little farther up the stream, easily managed measures readily control your course. The same holds for a female climax, but control of female orgasm is no great problem to most couples. The male can easily join in if he is ready and can generally hold out for a later, mutual climax if he is not. The first rule governing the sexual crescendo is thus that *the husband's tolerance at any one moment sets rigid limits upon degree of penetration and upon both his own and his wife's movement*. Any violation of this rule spoils the wife's chance of thorough satisfaction as well as shortening the husband's period of pleasurable transport, so that both parties gain by doing whatever is necessary to sustain the husband's capacities. You can accomplish this goal more easily through attention to two preliminaries:

1. *Both parties (but especially the husband) should learn the art of positive relaxation.*

Muscular tension is an integral part of sexual excitement. You can learn deliberately to resolve muscular tension in a few minutes. However, the height of sexual intercourse is no time to attempt this form of self-mastery for the first time. Best lie down alone in a quiet, darkened room and make yourself entirely comfortable. Learn how to decrease tightness of a muscle by working in the range with which you are already familiar—the range of deliberate muscular contraction. Hold your neck muscles a little bit stiff, then a bit stiffer, then quite stiff, then as stiff as possible. Now relax them again to quite stiff, moderately stiff, slightly stiff and normal. Another step in the same direction leads you into the realm of deliberate relaxation—of muscles loosened up even more than they are at ordinary rest. You will find that with a little practice you can relax muscles of one arm, one leg, the other leg, the other arm and so on until all your body parts are quite limp, then go back around the same succession of parts for even further relaxation. Do this several times a week until you can always relax your muscles quickly and deliberately, even when distractions make the task more difficult. If the husband applies this talent for relaxation whenever an imminent climax demands a pause in sexual activity, he will find it very effective indeed. Wifely relaxation at such times prevents the muscular quivers and pressures which might otherwise play a role in precipitating male orgasm.

2. *Set signals for a freeze.*

Especially when you first start on your sexual adjustment or readjustment, you need constant lines of couple communication. Some couples guide each other with steady murmuring as to their state. Utterances range from "That's the way— oh, that's what I like— you're really giving it to me tonight!" to more poetic comment, punctuated with kisses and caress. Other couples find talk is distracting, and let the husband signal for more or less movement with a guiding hand on his wife's hip or by making her match his own rhythmic action. Whatever your approach, a wife should always know when the husband wants a freeze, and should instantly heed his wishes. A calm discussion in an interval between sexual encounters may help make your signals more fruitful.

Maintaining feminine fervor.

The first few moments after penetration not only involve risk of a fast male climax but also prove the most likely time for waning wifely ardor. If the male indulges in long pauses to maintain his sexual control, the female gets little or no direct sexual stimulation. The contrast with intensive sex play just preceding makes this dearth of stimulation something of a letdown. The more passionate a woman, the more troublesome this period becomes. A slowly aroused wife generally responds gradually to sexual stimulations so that what counts to her is the average level over a period of minutes beforehand. The titillations just preceding sexual entrance continue to take effect throughout the man's first pause and keep her ardor on the rise. An easily aroused woman gets a prompt surge of sexual excitement with stimulation, and finds her excitement fading when stimulation ceases for more than a few minutes. Thus the second rule governing the sexual crescendo is that *both parties should do everything, short of movements which might bring on a male climax, to build and sustain the wife's ardor.*

Fortunately, many of the main centers of sexual sensitivity in women lie at or near the surface. Rubbing the sex organs together without penetration or short strokes with minimal penetration often gives the woman much more stimulation than the man. Women also gain considerable sexual excitement from stimulation of other areas besides the genitals, so that the husband can help to sustain his wife's ardor with kisses and mouth play or with caresses of the breasts, buttocks, thighs and back. The excitement which a woman derives from actively caressing her mate and from making her own sexual movements also deserves emphasis: too many women let sexual excitement die for want of expression, being too preoccupied with self-searching and too paralyzed by fear of frustration to let themselves go. The very act of caressing with the palms and with the mouth and performing active sexual movements often proves more exciting than even your partner's best attentions, especially to the passionate, fast-responding woman whose ardor fades quickly during lulls.

In spite of the husband's attentions and the wife's passionate activity, feminine fervor often wanes to a certain degree in the early moments of intercourse. If the woman becomes anxious about this reduction in passion, her anxiety usually kills whatever excitement she has left. Actually, she has no reason for anxiety: this waning of feeling will seldom interfere with her ultimate satisfaction or her husband's pleasure unless anxiety implements it.

In fact, the wife can usually turn the situation to real advantage by simply following her natural tendency toward playful withdrawal. She might writhe away from her husband slightly, give a husky laugh and nip him on the chest, then say: "Come on, chase me a little bit!" No man in his right mind would mistake such a retreat for rejection, especially if followed by a new flurry of bodily caresses. Both parties will savor a thrilling episode of further play, followed by an apt and thoroughly delightful union. However, the wife should not get truly beyond range, and should never lock her thighs, push her husband away, cover her genitals with her hands or take any other action which might suggest true evasion. She should tease by wiggling her hips as he tries to make a re-entry, by meeting his advance with a quick pinch on the low belly followed immediately with a wanton advance or a clinging caress, or by some other tantalizing combination of momentary interception with immediate caress. In other words, the third rule governing the sexual crescendo is that *a wife who finds that her husband's slow start in intercourse sometimes dampens her ardor should invoke an interval of advance-and-retreat play instead of forcing the pace*. A play interval excites both partners with no chance of causing a male climax, and turns each momentary lull into a positive advantage.

Prolonged periods of relative retreat.

If the husband's mood or nature makes teasing work out poorly, or if the waning of excitement has gone too far for salvage in this way, some couples find a period of relatively inactive sexual union helpful. The woman signals the man that urgency has passed for her. "Let's take it easy for a while," she says. They shift into a less strenuous position—roll on their sides, or shift the man around to the rear (which can be done without breaking sex contact by going through the wife's-heels-on-husband's-shoulders posture on the way), or go into the crossed posture. With murmured endearments, caresses and minimal movement, the man maintains his blissful transportation for some time. If the woman's interest perks back up (which it often does after five minutes or so) they resume activity immediately. If not, the man's mood and couple pacing through the months decide their course. Once the wife's passion has died down, she can readily give him her best without being caught halfway to a climax, and male completion does no harm. However, couples who must conserve masculine fervor to meet heavy feminine needs may prefer to let the man's passion also subside for the moment in hopes of resuming later. Phrased as a rule, you might say that *tapered sexual activity if the woman loses zeal often permits her husband to stay with her until another wave of passion rises in her breast, and always lets you resolve the crisis in a more or less satisfactory way.* Incidentally, the long pause on a mildly blissful plateau which results from following this rule not only gives most men considerable pleasure but also proves a good exercise for building sexual control and staying power. Some couples reach this state and then taper their sexual activity deliberately before seeking a climax, even spinning out the game through several nights. Neither party will suffer congestion or distress, if you simply keep up quiet activity long enough to let excitement subside naturally. The frantic push which most husbands start when their wives complain of waning excitement much more commonly leaves feminine congestion in its wake. The woman's urge cannot be reawakened so quickly, yet has not gently waned to leave her ready for either repose or loving service to her mate.

Sex movements and rhythms.

In most sex positions, the husband supplies the basic in-and-out movement by motions of his trunk. Instinct tells him to insert the penis to its full depth, then make fairly short, sharp motions a few seconds apart. Such movements will lead to quick release of sexual tension and often to a fairly satisfying climax. However, very few husbands can control biological pressure for more than a minute or so with this approach. The diffusion of sexual transport, in which the feeling of keen physical well-being spreads gradually through his entire body, never has a chance to develop. Neither does the true sexual self-mastery which leads to maximum wife-pleasing capability.

One simple change in sexual technique makes a tremendous difference: *The husband's base position in the early stages of intercourse should be at the withdrawal end of his stroke instead of at full penetration.* The main reason for this rule is that sexual control is much easier in this position, but several collateral benefits also result. If the woman's excitement wanes during one of her husband's pauses, she can draw away in playful retreat to resume surface rubbing together of the genitals (with the head of the penis between the outer lips instead of up inside the vagina) without causing frictions which might precipitate his climax. His first motions still remain quite comfortable for her even if her organs have not become completely relaxed and moist, since he does not reach full penetration for some time. The external base position permits a great deal of extra variety in movement, too, since the husband can easily change direction of his thrusts. By short, sharp strokes with the penis angled toward the very front of the vagina he can jolt the urinary tube, for instance. This sensitive passion trigger remains almost untouched in any motion he adopts with the penis all the way inside. Last but not least, your bodies remain sufficiently separated in the early moments of intercourse to allow continued fondling and caress of the clitoris and other sensitive spots during the less active early stages when feminine ardor otherwise might wane.

A second change in technique from the instinctive

which many men find helpful substitutes *long, slow strokes with which the wife can coordinate her movements for short, sharp ones which she cannot supplement*. Most couples find the long, slow stroke many times as satisfying even in positions which prevent feminine cooperation, since sexual stimulation comes in a sustained wave instead of a quick blip. Slow movement stimulates exactly the way a longer organ would—"as if all of a sudden I was in bed with a sexual giant, but without any uncomfortable stretching" was one wife's description of the change. Perhaps at the start of activity, when you need a fairly long interval between strokes to keep from spurring a male climax, a few rocking motions during the intervals will help to sustain feminine excitement. Other measures like deliberate genital twitchings discussed later in this chapter work well in conjunction with long strokes, too.

Lastly, most men find themselves more effective as wifepleasers if they *think of the penis as a rasp instead of a punch*. You can draw the shaft of the penis along the clitoris with much more effect if you lift the shaft against this sensitive structure than if you think only of the movements at the tip. The same holds for other sexual frictions, which mainly originate where the penis rubs past the woman's sexual opening instead of deep inside.

The wife's sex movements.

Feminine contributions to sexual frictions mainly take an entirely different form, with the wife's genital membranes usually sliding across or around the penis rather than along its axis. A wife gains purchase for her movements by keeping her heels on the bed or hooked behind her husband's knees, by locking her feet behind his back, or by getting into an astride posture. She rocks her pelvis forward in a sort of burlesque bump and rocks it backward in a sway-backed genital retreat. At first, this motion should not be combined with the husband's in-and-out stroke on a one-for-one basis—as long as his strokes remain slow and deliberate, her movements can match his on a three- or four-to-one basis so that her organ describes a zigzag course along the shaft of his penis during each advance and retreat. Later, when the climax grows quite close, some couples shift to a syncopated or simple one-for-one rhythm, while others find the woman's short sharp motion combined with the man's long slide more satisfying all the way to the end.

By combining the front-to-back rock with similar movement up and down on the bed, you can achieve a circular motion which produces quite exquisite sexual frictions. The term "screwing" gives a very false picture of this action. Female movement does not twirl the vagina in a horizontal axis while the penis moves in and out in a vertical one. The woman's motions remain entirely in the front-to-back plane with virtually no sidewise element. She may move her vagina in a circle, but all elements of that motion are lengthwise or up and down to her body axis, like the edge of an imaginary dinner plate stood up between closed thighs. You can accomplish this movement quite easily in standard wife-on-her-back posture by pushing yourself up toward the head of the bed with your legs during each forward movement with your trunk muscles, and letting your body recoil toward the foot of the bed as your hips drop. Three or four quick rolls to each slow male stroke makes a good starting rhythm. A wife's complete circle to match each of her husband's strokes and withdrawals also makes for interesting sensations.

Movement of the genitals themselves.

You can learn to move and control certain muscles in your genital area which make possible independent movement of the genitals. Twitching these muscles during ordinary sexual motions or during rest periods adds charming variety and intensity to the stimulations which you give to your partner. An added advantage for wives and mothers is the restoration of muscle tone in a birth-stretched vagina by the control-establishing exercises. Why not work toward muscular control by yourself until you have developed a degree of facility, then surprise your partner with it?

Genital twitching in the man results from contraction of muscles at the base of the penile shaft about two inches in front of the rectum. You contract these muscles when you try to lift your testicles and scrotum straight up into your body. If the penis is not erect, it will not move when you carry out this motion (and neither will the testicles, of course). You can check whether the right muscles are contracting by pressing one finger up into your flesh just at the rear attachment of the scrotum. Short, sharp twitches of this muscle body give the greatest effect. Once you have learned the action, you can practice without pushing your finger into the flesh, since the sensation you get from contracting the proper muscles is quite distinctive. You can snap the muscle a few times while you are driving your car or sitting in an office or any place you happen to think of it, both building muscular strength and learning instant control.

When you use this action during intercourse, try it first during pauses and rest intervals. A few jolts will help your wife to maintain her ardor, without speeding your own climax at all. Next try snapping once or twice at the depth of penetration on ordinary sex strokes. When you have mastered muscular control thoroughly, try snapping the penis two or three times during an ordinary slow stroke or continuing to snap it in rapid runs through several cyclic sex movements.

A woman can learn several different types of genital movement, and can combine them in many different ways. The easiest motion to learn follows when you try to pull the vagina straight up into your body. This motion, like the husband's genital twitch, enlivens both sexual pauses and moments of active friction if applied in short, sharp spasms. A similar but slightly different effect comes when you attempt to pull the rectum up into your body. You can practice both these movements any time and any place, since they involve no external manifestations.

Mastery of the muscles around the vagina itself calls for more concentrated effort. You can generally contract these muscles by trying to squeeze with the vagina itself (not in a straining motion like that used to evacuate the bowels), perhaps by pretending that you are trying to pick up marbles with it. The resulting contraction helps to make you a more pleasing sexual partner even if you never perform it during intercourse, especially if childbirth has stretched the tissues out of shape. It helps build up tone in the muscles for snugger fit and greater natural action. Several contractions in a row on three or four occasions each day usually make a real difference to your sexual proficiency within a few weeks. The habit of contracting the vaginal muscles a few times before you get up in the morning helps to maintain your capacities thereafter.

After mastering simple contraction of the vagina, a few women go on to learn wave-like contraction beginning at the outer opening and proceeding up inside the organ. Like the muscle control by which you govern bladder action, this form of bodily skill calls for mastery of muscles whose ordinary action is involuntary. Some women can never learn this action, and most must work at it for several weeks or months. If you want to learn this skill, try first to achieve vaginal contraction just at the female opening, then let the contraction flow on up the passage. If you succeed in practice, use this action just before and during your husband's sex climax to earn his keenest appreciation.

Caresses during intercourse.

In most positions, you can supplement the effect of sexual frictions with a number of caresses. The wife can almost always reach sexually sensitive areas of her husband's body with her hands during intercourse. The husband finds himself somewhat restricted in many positions by the necessity for supporting his body weight, but can occasionally work at least one hand free in virtually every posture.

Light, brushing caresses of the ear lobes, hair and shoulders help to express your affection during the early part of intercourse. Stroking caresses of the wife's buttocks with either up-and-down, side-to-side or rotary friction seem especially apt during the next phase. Both sexes respond to stroking of the thighs and lower abdomen in positions which permit free access to these parts. As the final surge approaches, kneading or muscle-clutching caresses bring excitement to a lofty peak. The shift from stroking of the buttock or thigh to a deeper, somewhat rougher muscle-clutching caress actually does more to bring many couples to climax than any change in sexual frictions themselves, and very effectively increases sexual excitement.

How to apply this chapter's guidance
in managing your own sexual crescendo.

Your first sexual contact during intercourse should involve relatively little penetration. Immediately after entry, you should pause until the husband feels that he has complete mastery of biological pressures. He should then try a few tentative, short strokes, always returning to a position of minimal penetration instead of leaving the organs in deep contact. During this period, both parties should continue kissing and stroking caresses. Teasing is not only an exciting part of sexual sport at this stage, but also provides the best means with which the wife can encourage a bit more play whenever she strikes an emotional lull. She makes her husband chase her a bit, at the same time exchanging a few mischievous caresses with him, without in any way disturbing his pleasure. In fact, both partners usually become more excited in this way without the problems of control which her husband would encounter if he tried to rebuild his wife's excitement through sexual frictions. In prolonging sex play with teasing, however, you should always make sure that your words and gestures carry no hint of true rejection or denial. Make your husband chase you as much as you want, but make sure he knows all the time that you want to be caught.

If you find teasing poorly suited to either partner's temperament, or if the loss of feminine fervor gets too far before you recognize the need for further play, the wife should signal her husband to take it easy for a while. By quiet sexual motions and gentle sex play, you can prolong relations on a pleasant plateau for a period of time. Women often feel some reawakening of sensual excitement after such a relaxing lull, and men lose absolutely nothing in satisfaction (and gain substantially in sexual control through the experience). If the wife's interest does not revive, she can quite comfortably finish off her husband's love rite without any risk of being left high. Or the husband can choose to let his own excitement settle down over a period of time and save his capacity for a more fruitful occasion.

After a few slow strokes and perhaps a pause or two for relaxation, the husband's biological pressures should subside. Usually, he will feel a spread of feeling like a warm glow or a bodily lightness from the genitals to every part of his body, and the sense of genital urgency which previously made control difficult then disappears. At this point, deeper penetration involves no risks. Rhythmic couple movements intensify the feeling of sexual transport without bringing a quick climax, and the woman can begin to reap her harvest. In early episodes, the man can set his own rhythm with slow, long strokes coupled with short jolts and perhaps occasionally with snapping of the penis through muscular contraction at its base. Writhing from side to side with the shaft of his penis jammed up against the clitoris gives his wife an extra thrill without speeding his own progress. The wife can move in quivers or jerks while lying on her side or in grinding and rocking motions while astride without

causing loss of control or contact. She can lift or contract her vagina in rhythmic pulses without other
bodily movement in any sex position. Both partners
can use deepstroking and muscle-clutching caress to
speed progress toward a climax, or sustain excitement
with milder measures. You can enjoy breast play during intercourse in most positions, too, and can devote
considerable attention to the buttocks or thighs. After
mastering the basic sexual skills, you can try synchronizing your couple movements, at first with three or
four female pulses to each long, slow, masculine stroke,
later with other rhythms and variations.

6.
The Fifth Key to Soundly Satisfying Sex: A Deliberately Heightened Climax

Until the penis begins to twitch in an involuntary seizure, you can always choose whether you want to prolong or intensify your sexual communion. But the first sign of orgastic paroxysm in the male means intercourse is due to end, and you might as well end it rousingly.

Climactic movements.

Most couples finish off in the wife-on-her-back posture at first, even when they have stayed in another posture throughout the earlier stages of the episode. In this position, the husband's instinctive movements prove quite effective. The wife's instinctive movements also contribute during moments of passionate transport. Most brides instinctively hold their backs almost rigid as they bounce up and down in bed at climax time, almost withdrawing their genitals beyond the husband's range. Their hips tend to roll back into the position which would be ideal for approach from the rear, coinciding with the primitive mammalian pattern, rather than forward into position for face-to-face union. This primitive response should not be confused with withdrawal, nor need you alter it deliberately. The uncurbed ardor thus expressed means much more to early marriage or sexual rehabilitation than any technical refinements.

Most wives develop their proficiency at climax time mainly on occasions which they carry out in loving service rather than on occasions involving animal ardor. All action is deliberate on husband-serving occasions, so that planned motion and deliberate experiment involve no unnatural distraction. After you have mastered a certain sexual maneuver during husband-serving occasions, you will find that you can carry it out with mutual advantage and without loss of ardor during even the keenest passionate transportation.

The synchronous rocking or rolling motions of the earlier stage prove quite effective at climax time if you adopt a somewhat livelier rhythm. The main muscles used are those of the buttocks rather than the abdomen or spine, and the body action rolls the genital area in a back-to-front arc rather than lifting the whole body off the bed. By keeping one or both hands on your husband's hips, you can usually stay in some kind of rhythm with him even at his most rapid peak —three or four rocks for each thrust if he keeps a slow beat, one or two if he speeds up faster, or even one for each three or four thrusts if he takes to short and rapid strokes.

Climactic genital twitches.

Twitching of the penis through contraction of the muscles at its base, as described in the last chapter, precisely duplicates the final paroxysms of a male

orgasm. After a woman has come to link this motion
with keen sexual delight through several episodes of
sexual success, her husband can often boost her along
with voluntary twitchings. If your wife goes into
orgasm before you are entirely ready for a mutual
climax, this trick will intensify her pleasure considerably.

Actual motion pictures taken inside a woman's
vagina during orgasm show that intense waves of
muscular motion pass along the female tube during
each final climax. The build-up of musculature accomplished by the exercises recommended in the last
chapter undoubtedly makes those natural movements
more intensive with increased satisfaction to both
parties (especially to the husband). However, there is
no need to contract the vagina deliberately during a
mutually orgastic episode: nature accomplishes this
goal for you.

On the other hand, a run of lifting-type muscular
contractions sends an extra pulse of feeling through
both partners, and adds very pleasant variety to either
a husband-serving or a mutual climax. Like most skills
exerted at this time, you should probably perform
these motions when you are being helpful instead of
when you are driven by passion before trying it in
more ardent moments. However, after a little practice
the action becomes so natural that you will not find it
particularly distracting.

Both straight contraction of the female tube and
wavelike voluntary movement can heighten the male
climax during episodes of loving service. In fact, many
women find their ability to please their husbands so
increased by these maneuvers that reflected gratification combined with pride in sexual achievement sometimes become more important than orgasm to them,

and they may occasionally undertake husband-pleasing efforts by preference to uninhibitedly passionate ones. The effectiveness of this sacrifice has been attested by several noted courtesans, who almost invariably quenched their climactic ardor during intercourse with their royal sponsors in order to perform with greater skill.

Climactic caresses.

Your sex climax comes about through stimulation of nerve endings, most of which are identical with pain fibers in your skin. The few non-pain nerves respond to temperature change rather than to touch or pressure. Therefore, caresses which stimulate pain nerves in sexually sensitive areas actually boost your climax more effectively than any others.

A stinging *slap* on the back or buttock makes a most effective climactic caress. Without being so heavy handed as to risk injuring your partner, you can get a broad area of his skin tingling with climax-boosting nervous discharge in this way. Raking his back and thighs with your fingernails has a similar effect.

Many women respond very keenly to *horse-bite-like clutching* of the buttocks or thighs just at their sexual climax.

Love-nips of the neck, shoulder and chest, or *pinches* of the abdomen, buttocks and thighs sometimes spur members of either sex to new heights.

Surface-layer pinches of the scrotum sac spur many husbands along the path to ecstasy and can make the crucial moment maddeningly intense.

Many of these caresses border upon injury and call for reasonable restraint. Your partner's feelings are no guide, since the direct effect of these caresses at the spot caressed often seems unpleasant. Your partner may draw away or squeal resentfully even while the sexual pleasures which your slap or pinch excites brings him or her to ever-expanding ecstasy. Like a cold plunge on a hot day, the stimulation is often worth the initial shock, and you must judge from the total effect on your partner's sexual response rather than from his or her impression of the particular means you choose to cap his climax.

Celebration specials.

After a few months of well-conceived sexual adjustment, you will find that most episodes yield fairly intense satisfaction. Different positions and approaches keep these pleasures fresh. But occasionally, one of you (especially the husband) will yearn for something special—something different, something intense, something to reawaken sexual interest and enthusiasm in marriage. If your partner shows signs of tapering enthusiasm or slow arousal, or if you just want to give him a special thrill on some festive occasion, a climax-boosting trick may prove worthwhile. These tricks all involve some element which makes them impractical for everyday sex life. They usually require attentions too complex to give while in the grips of passion, so that you must be willing to give up much of your delight to supplement your partner's, and a few will seem definitely improper to people of certain upbringing. If you use these techniques at all, I would strongly suggest that you stick to two rules:

1. *Use only those techniques which seem proper to you without trying to talk yourself into them.*
There's no sense getting into something which will

fill you with revulsion because of deeply implanted social taboos even if you know intellectually that those taboos are senseless.

2. *Never ask or expect your partner to apply these special measures.*

They should be one hundred per cent spontaneous and voluntary at all times.

With these limitations, you might find use for these techniques once in a lifetime or once or twice a year (but probably not more often than that unless your sex pace is very rapid indeed).

Couples who have relations several times each week have more trouble working in enough variety to keep the thrills of sex life fresh. As one client phrased it: "We've had relations every way but hanging from the chandelier, and still we're going stale with one another." For such couples, techniques which ordinary pairs should keep for very rare occasions might prove necessary every month or two.

The ice-spurred special.

Freezing cold against your skin stimulates both pain and temperature nerves, which are exactly the types of fiber which trigger your sex climax. The ice-spurred special takes advantage of this fact. Before intercourse, the wife places at the bedside a bowl of crushed ice or a handful of cracked ice wrapped in a wet towel. Both partners strip and enjoy sex in any face-to-face posture with the husband on top. As the husband starts his final surge to climax, the wife picks up a handful of crushed ice or the cold towel. Just as the paroxysms of orgasm start, she jams the ice-cold poultice against her husband's crotch and keeps it there throughout his conclusion.

The ice-spurred special works well in reverse also, with the wife astride and the husband performing the maneuver. In this position, however, the technique calls for a perfectly timed, mutual climax: the icy flood involves the husband as it cascades off the wife, and often upsets his erection-maintaining balance if it hits too early. If you use ice on a preliminary female orgasm or if your timing sometimes is a bit off, use a method which avoids run-off. You can chill your hand in the ice bowl, then boost your wife's climax with the frigid hand instead of with the ice itself, for instance.

Urinary passage pressure.

As the husband hits his absolute peak, the wife can press her bunched fingertips firmly into his flesh just at the back of his scrotum in a harsh goosing jiggle. The main jets of his ejaculation lie in the urinary passage at this site, and the impact of those jets upon the urinary tube accounts for much of his climactic sensation. Pressure upon this spot sends him on an ecstatic whirl.

After a few months of married life, the urinary passage also has intense sexual sensitivity in most women. The husband can press urinary organs which could not otherwise be touched (and portions of the vagina which rarely get direct stimulation) down into range of the surging penis with a special maneuver. Toward the end of intercourse in the wife's-heels-on-husband's-shoulders posture, he puts one hand against her lower abdomen just above the pubic bone and presses firmly down toward the pelvis, pushing her abdominal wall and attached structures down toward the inner end of her female organ. As his wife hits her climax, a rapid rotary movement of his hand adds further to her delight.

Subsidence.

There's an old saying that he who hits and runs away lives to fight another day. The wisdom of leaving the encounter unfinished also applies occasionally to sex. In couples where feminine passion runs high and the man's normal sexual capacity barely meets his wife's requirement for orgasms, the waste of masculine capacity in a one-sided climax often leaves her with unmet needs later in the month. Subsidence without a male climax leaves the husband ready for further service soon.

Sexual excitement usually proceeds in waves, building and subsiding until it reaches a high peak from which abrupt subsidence through orgasm leaves you utterly replete. However, any high-peaked wave will pass and leave a trough of subsiding feeling, provided stimulation does not bring another wave into being before the first dies down.

If you plan an episode with gradual subsidence (which some couples find quite satisfying as a sort of dress rehearsal for orgastic sex), you probably should try it first on a holiday morning: holiday because you need to take as much time as nature demands, and morning because the best way to keep from getting excited again immediately is usually to get out of bed and busy yourself with other things. A casual brush against your partner's thigh during the night will otherwise revive your interest with a bang, before your partner hardly gets a chance to get awake.

Approach from the rear while lying on your sides has some advantages for long-sustained contact, although some couples lie face to face in order to enjoy more conversation and caress. Take your long pause and early, lightly penetrating motions until you have biological pressures well in hand, then sustain yourself on the plateau of sexual transport for several minutes. At first, most couples cannot hold an erection for more than three or four minutes without more motion than the male can tolerate, but many ultimately achieve very prolonged union. After a few minutes, you will feel impelled toward increased movement, an interval of advance-and-retreat sex play or some other form of enlivening caress. If you resist this impulse, it will gradually subside and a wave of torpor will begin to overtake you. At this point, you can cease sex motions and withdraw partly or all the way. Soothing caresses in slow tempo may help to build your incipient torpor. When you feel fully calmed, break contact. A leisurely, lukewarm tub bath helps to quiet any left-over excitement for you.

Afterplay.

Some couples consider the afterglow of a mutually orgasic episode one of its most pleasant elements. They linger in conversation, intimate embraces and caress for an hour or more after intercourse. Others find the desire for sleep overwhelming, and separate after a few moments of murmured appreciation. Either course is perfectly satisfactory after true and mutual passionate release.

On less ideally harmonious occasions, long afterplay actually seems more essential. A woman who has conferred her favor without orgasmic reward gets most of her gratification through her husband's response. The least he can do is to communicate his feelings in embraces and caress, and perhaps in murmurs of appreciation and regard. A woman who has built up a head of passion which her husband was unable to requite deserves a further push to climax through intensive genital caress, or (if she has not come quite close enough for that) a prolonged period of embrace and gentle caress designed to let her down easy.

As soon as the climax has passed, touch nerves resume importance. Climactic caresses, which stir pain fibers, become inept. Afterplay is gentle, slow in rhythm, with few surprises and no games of coquetry or retreat. Surface stroking and soft kisses play more part than violent, excitement-building frictions.

How to put this chapter's methods to work for you.

Once a male climax begins, you might as well boost it along with instinctive or deliberate movements and caress. Both husband and wife should give their body movements free rein during early passion-spurred climaxes. The woman should learn refinements during episodes of sexual service rather than ungovernable ardor. At such times, she should try to replace instinctive lunging or stiff-backed bouncing with rocking or rolling movement of her hips. In positions allowing synchronous couple movement, she should keep one hand on her husband's hip or buttock as a guide to his rhythm. Most couples find that a slow, long male stroke with several female pulses along its course gives a fascinating beat, but dozens of different rhythms are possible.

After a little preliminary practice, most husbands

and wives can learn to twitch, lift or squeeze the genitals independently of body movement. These techniques help during all stages of intercourse, but lead to especially helpful stimulations at the climax. The woman gains sexual proficiency from practicing certain of these movements even if she does not consciously apply them during intercourse, since the exercise-strengthened muscles contract automatically during her instinctive spasms.

Just as your hands should remain busy throughout the crescendo, so should they also heighten your partner's climax (and your own). Non-injuring methods of stimulating pain nerves such as the slap, the scratch, horse-bite-like clutching, love-nips, and pinches add stimulation identical to that provided by genital friction. On a few special occasions (not too frequently, because these should be big events), you can use either ice or urinary passage pressure for an ecstatically-boosted sex climax, provided neither of you considers these maneuvers beyond the pale.

Instead of boosting the climax, you may sometimes decide to replace it with tapering, soothing embrace. Episodes which the wife conducts out of loving service or occasions on which she is left high require extra usbandly attention, either in loving embrace and expression of gratitude, in orgasm-producing supplemental stimulation, or in tapering love play. The quiet, much-loved feeling of after-intercourse embrace deserves enjoyment, too. Don't leave this pleasure undiscovered by *always* going right to sleep.

7.
How to
Free Each Other
of Sexual Fears and
Emotional Restraints

If you suffer as a couple from frequent or continual difficulty in your sex life, you must almost always attack linkages of disruptive emotion with intercourse. Unpleasant emotional overtones frequently cast a deep pall over a couple's entire physical relationship, completely blocking a wife's response or making a husband literally impotent. Even if fear or guilt never put you under profound constraint, they may impair your response enough that release from emotional burdens will genuinely improve your sexual gratifications.

If you and your partner stiffen up emotionally in anticipation of sex or during intimate sex play, you unquestionably have a great deal to gain by ridding yourselves of emotional constraint. But whether you stiffen up or not, the principal fears and upheavals connected with sex deserve attention. Almost every couple can gain by dealing directly and effectively with fear of pregnancy, fear of sexual injury, fear of failure or inadequacy, and guilt arising from subconscious application of unsuitable taboos and restrictions.

Fear of pregnancy.

Every woman alive has some aversion to certain aspects of pregnancy, even if she also has an overwhelming desire to be a mother. The unpleasant emotional tone which this fear attaches to sexual union distinctly dampens feminine ardor in many (if not most) marriages.

You can decrease the effect of such unspoken dread in your own marriage by bringing it out into the open where you can deal with it rationally. Here's a step by step program:

Acknowledge that fear of pregnancy plagues you, as it plagues virtually every woman.

Once in a while, I have to break the news of pregnancy to a prospective mother. Most women say: "That's what I was afraid of!" and give a wry grin. Even when one acts overjoyed, her later actions usually show that pregnancy was less than totally welcome.

Regardless of the reams of romantic propaganda about motherhood, this reaction is perfectly natural. Pregnancy involves complete change in your life plans, distinct physical discomforts and disabilities, a period of unattractiveness which challenges your marriage, rumored alterations in capacity to please your husband (which mainly fail to materialize with proper care during pregnancy and slight alterations in technique afterward) and a small but definite mortal risk.

Concern about the possibility of pregnancy is as normal to a married woman as fear of bullets to a soldier in battle. A wife doesn't have to deny her fear or rid herself of it in order to enjoy sex or undertake motherhood. Like the soldier, she usually does better by acknowledging her fear and letting other emotions, desires and loyalties overwhelm it. In this way, she can take whatever actions are logical to quell her dread, mobilize emotional support and help which denial would not permit, and bring her feelings into proper proportion through the action of her own good sense and knowledge.

STEP ONE: *Talk over your family plans to counteract fear of pregnancy.*

While positive feeling in favor of a pregnancy cannot uproot fear altogether, it can help you to overcome that emotion. If you decide to pursue motherhood after you have thoroughly discussed the subject, that discussion itself will have crystallized the affirmative feelings which help you to combat pregnancy dread. If you decide together to use some means of delaying pregnancy, you will still have brought out the plus factors of child rearing in the course of your discussion, and can recall them easily as needed. And you will have laid the groundwork for cooperative couple measures to reduce the chance of pregnancy, through which your fears should be substantially reduced.

STEP TWO: *Conception control if required by either your situation or your emotional state.*

Several methods substantially reduce the likelihood that intercourse will result in pregnancy, and should therefore help quell the woman's fears. If religious considerations prevent you from using chemical or mechanical means of birth control, systems based on confining intercourse to the less fertile portions of the woman month offer your only recourse. With an ordinary twenty-eight-day cycle, you should refrain from relations from the ninth to the nineteenth day (counting the first day of menstrual flow as Day One). If your cycle usually proves longer or shorter than the standard one, check the list below for your proper denial days:

If your cycle is Days Long,	give up intercourse from Day to Day:	
21	2	12
22	3	13
23	4	14
24	5	15
25	6	16
26	7	17
27	8	18
28	9	19
29	10	20
30	11	21
31	12	22
32	13	23
33	14	24
34	15	25
35	16	26

These figures allow two days' latitude each way for slight irregularity. If your cycle varies more than two days from its average, you might extend the unsafe period by a day or two. With very irregular periods, rhythm methods generally fail.

You can reduce fertility to a bit under half its usual level with the ordinary rhythm method, so long as

periods are fairly regular. Some couples can do even
better by checking the wife's temperature each day
before she stirs around in the morning. The temperature usually hangs at a certain level for a few days
after menstruation, then dips half a degree for one day
and settles thereafter at a level a half degree or so
above the before-the-dip base. Your egg cell breaks
loose at the time of the dip (or the shift in base temperature if the dip is not very distinct). By allowing
four days before and five days after this dip as safety
margin, you can suit period control to your own
biologic rhythm. Don't get discouraged if no dip ap-
pears the first month—quite a few women have some
cycles without ovulation, and the temperature curve
during such cycles shows no dip. Usually, you get a
good enough picture from following the temperature
through two dip-revealing months to quit taking tem-
peratures thereafter.

If your religious convictions impose no limitations
on birth control methods, three additional techniques deserve consideration. Failures do occur, sometimes in the very first month, but on the average each
of these methods limits pregnancies to one for each
twenty years of cohabitation. You can cut the failure
rate further by combining chemical means with
rhythm, as described in the last section, if your sex
pace permits.

1. *Rubbers.*

Couples react differently to intercourse with a
rubber in place. Some compare it to a shower in a
raincoat. Others find it acceptable if somewhat muted.
A few find dulling of male perception by the layer
of rubber helpful in permitting the husband to hold
out until the wife's climax, while others find that the

wife's satisfaction depends to a large degree on impact of the jets of semen which the rubber interrupts. The gap in sex play occasioned by need to don the rubber after erection causes no problems for some couples but upsets others badly. Among my own patients, very few choose rubbers for general use after trying the other techniques, although quite a few use rubbers for an occasional episode. Rubbers provide instantly available protection in case an urge gets so far along that suppositories would not have time to melt, or develops when the diaphragm is not in place. You can keep one in your wallet (well wrapped to avoid puncture) in case a sex urge arises away from home. Rubbers often prove the most acceptable method for conception control during menstrual flow. The stimulations which come through a rubber seem sufficiently different to add variety even if they do not prove intensely satisfying, and some couples change off with them occasionally for this reason alone.

Most failures of conception control with rubbers come through splitting. You can usually avoid this problem by unrolling and collapsing a turn or two of slack at the end of the penis before rolling the rubber on up the shaft. Second engagements have some hazards after using a rubber, since sperm on skin surfaces can live for several hours without losing their punch. You should probably wash off the penis and the hands before resuming intimate sex play when you use this birth control technique.

2. *Diaphragms.*

Most newlyweds get good results with diaphragm-and-jelly birth control. The wife can make her preparations every night when she gets ready for bed, avoiding any interruption in sex play. The diaphragm does not interfere with sexual frictions on the penis or on the clitoris and female opening. Most wives have a great deal of confidence in the diaphragm, and the ritual by which it is fitted and used helps to reinforce that feeling.

You should get a diaphragm fitted by your physician or in a Planned Parenthood Clinic instead of using a "universal size" (which actually may fit you quite poorly) from a drugstore. The doctor who does the fitting should give you detailed instructions on insertion and use. Ideally he will let you insert the diaphragm before or during a recheck examination to be sure that you know how to do it and that the size is right when you are relaxed (which you may not be during your first visit).

In using the diaphragm, you should adopt the Boy Scout motto and always *be prepared*. Most failures occur when the wife feels tired or out of sorts, doesn't see any prospects for sex, and leaves her diaphragm in the dresser drawer. Then an eager husband or an unexpected impulse overcomes her lethargy and pregnancy results.

Although the directions say to use jelly only at the time when the diaphragm is inserted, I would advise you to apply a further charge of jelly in a vaginal applicator (which you can get at any drugstore) or with your finger just before any second engagements and any time the diaphragm has been in place for more than three hours—*always* before morning encounters. Make sure that your doctor shows you how to feel for the mouth of your womb through the dome of your diaphragm while he is fitting it, and get in the habit of checking this point *every time* after inserting the equipment. The hesitation many women feel about putting a finger into the vagina for this purpose usually goes back to childhood warnings against self-injury rather than to plain prudishness, and often disappear when they keep their fingernails trimmed short, use a little jelly for lubricant, or use a rubber finger stall to keep the nails from scratching delicate tissues. If you need any artificial lubricants during intercourse while wearing a diaphragm, use K-Y jelly or some other glycerine-base lubricant, since petroleum jelly quickly rots rubber.

After two weeks of marriage and again after three months, you should arrange to have your diaphragm checked and possibly refitted. Stretching of the vagina in sexual relations changes the size substantially during the introductory period. Further rechecks once a year may also prove worthwhile.

Although a diaphragm usually does not impair the wife's sexual sensitivity during the early months of marriage, it definitely blocks off friction from certain areas which become important sources of gratification after six months to a year. If you experiment with other means of control about every six months, you may find after a time that you strongly prefer another method. While a few of my patients stick with the diaphragm all the way through, most ultimately adopt suppositories or jellies either all the time or for a few extra-pleasant episodes in the less fertile phases of the woman month.

3. *Suppositories and jellies.*

You will find suppositories or jellies very simple to use, almost devoid of effect on sexual frictions and stimulations, relatively inexpensive and quite convenient. Actual measurement of their efficiency shows that they protect about as well as the diaphragm as ordinarily used (although not quite as well as a uniformly inserted diaphragm whose position has been checked on every occasion with an inserted finger and whose charge of jelly has been refreshed before intercourse if necessary).

On the other hand some couples find troublesome the necessity for taking specific precautions immediately before intercourse or working the precautions into their early love play, especially while maidenly modesty persists. Others find at least some of the recommended products too lubricating, so that sexual frictions seem less pleasurable with their use. Suppositories melt in very hot weather unless kept in the refrigerator. Neither suppositories nor jellies can be kept along with you for ready use on spontaneous occasions outside of your own home or in non-bedroom situations.

The key points in deciding between a diaphragm and suppositories or jellies alone usually are the extent of impairment of the wife's sensation by the diaphragm (which generally is almost none at first, but may increase as time goes on), the effect of interruption in sex play or need to anticipate the build-up of sexual excitement, and the degree of faith you have in each method. All of these elements vary for each couple, so you will have to appraise them for yourself. If you want to give jellies or suppositories a try, you should be able to get one of the following brands at your drugstore without a prescription:

Suppositories:
  Lorophyn
  Phe-Mer-Nite
  Vagagill

Jellies or creams:
    Delfen Vaginal Cream*
    Immolin Vaginal Cream-Jel*
    Lanesta Jelly*
    Ramses Vaginal Jelly*
    Koromex Vaginal Jelly
    Lorophyn Jelly
    Preceptin Vaginal Gel
    Vagagill Jelly

If you choose a suppository, unwrap it before insertion. Some brands have heavy foil packaging which can be torn through in such a way that the suppository can be squeezed out in a matter of moments. Others have a foil inner wrap which you will find frustrating if left until sex play is in progress, and which can safely be removed in advance so long as the suppository does not get warm enough to melt afterward. The foil will keep it in shape when it is softened by warmth, so that a dip in cold water prior to unwrapping will restore its consistency. Insert the suppository a finger's length into the vagina either beforehand or in the course of sex play. Most suppositories take about fifteen minutes to melt completely. If fast-moving preliminaries get you ready for contact before the suppository has definitely had time to melt, the husband should check with his finger during genital play to make sure that it is fairly well dispersed before commencing intercourse. Use another suppository for second engagements or if you break off for an hour or so before resuming activity.

If you use a jelly, you will need an applicator.

---

* I particularly recommend these preparations, which contain an exceedingly effective spermicidal agent.

Usually this consists of a hollow tube which can be screwed to the tube of jelly and a plunger which fits inside. With the plunger all the way down, you screw the applicator onto the tube. Press enough jelly into the applicator to fill it to the mark. The jelly pushes the plunger out ahead of it. You should usually make this much of your preparation in advance, although you may or may not want to go ahead with insertion of the jelly. Either before commencing sex play or during its latter stages, insert the applicator deep into the vagina and press the plunger to desposit a charge of jelly near the mouth of the womb. The plastic applicator will not stand boiling and dissolves in alcohol, so you should wash it in warm, soapy water between uses.

Jellies spread rapidly in the vagina. You can go ahead with intercourse as soon as you wish after application. Use a fresh charge for repeat engagements or if you wait an hour or more after insertion of the jelly before commencing intercourse.

4. *Tablets.*

The first kind of birth control tablets to become generally available work by keeping egg cells from completely ripening. You must take the tablets for several weeks to establish their effect. A gap in your schedule makes action uncertain for a week or more, so that you must use the tablets even when intercourse seems unlikely. If you keep rigidly to your prescribed schedule, however, tablets work at least as well as other methods of conception control, and possibly a bit better.

Several points favor tablets over other means of birth control. Tablets work quite reliably. They interfere in no way with couple enjoyment of sex. The wife takes care of everything herself, leaving no reason to fear a pregnancy through any careless or deliberate omission by her husband. All barriers of time and place collapse in husband-wife relations—there's no need for equipment or supplies to keep sex confined to the bedroom, and no worry about whether precautions taken hours earlier will protect you in the middle of the night or in the morning.

Tablets are not an unmixed blessing, however. You can only get them on prescription, which means one or two visits to your doctor each year. They cost a good deal more than other birth control techniques, even if you don't count the extra doctor bills. The tablets profoundly alter an important body function, which could conceivably lead to harmful effects with prolonged use or in a few sensitive individuals even, although tests to date seem to show reasonable safety.

Tablets with other modes of action have had less extensive but still substantial trial. One variety keeps the fertilized egg cell from attaching itself within the uterus. Another interferes with the sperm's penetration of the egg. These tablets cost a good deal less than ovulation-suppressors, but are not as readily available.

If you are interested in birth control tablets, why not discuss the situation with your doctor? He knows the latest facts, and can fit them to your individual sexual and economic needs. And if tablets seem the proper answer, he can write a prescription for you on the spot.

5. *Combinations of methods.*

When a woman feels strong fear or aversion to pregnancy, she often cannot take full satisfaction from one method of conception control, especially one which involves relatively little ritual. The failure of a certain method within her circle of acquaintance may also impair her faith. In such circumstances, a combination of diaphragm, suppository or jelly with period control may prove a real help. Added refinements such as a fresh charge of jelly inserted with an applicator during sex play in addition to the usual diaphragm technique and basal temperature checks in addition to ordinary rhythm often prove reassuring. Try to avoid combinations which include a rubber, if possible, since these generally impair satisfaction quite a bit.

While most husbands feel somewhat impatient with the folderol and clutter involved in multiple methods, these elements actually add to the wife's assurance. Most couples find some combination which sets the wife at ease without impairing satisfaction gravely, and a year or two of successful conception control generally lets fear die down sufficiently to make a modified program acceptable.

STEP THREE: *Keep an alternate family plan ready to make pregnancy less fearsome.*

While you would think that any mention of possible pregnancy might increase the violence of a woman's pregnancy fears, the opposite is usually the case. Concern about how the bills can be paid if she quits work, where she can put another crib in the small apartment, and so on, actually lie beneath much of her fear. When she can see in black and white how life could go on with decency and respect (and it almost always can) with one more child, much of her fear of pregnancy often vanishes. Besides making a better welcome for the child in case of a slip, you will find that a concrete plan covering exactly what you will do for space, money and facilities will usually decrease the fearsomeness of this prospect.

STEP FOUR: *After the menopause, ask your doctor for a definite opinion on your fertility.*

After the menopause has definitely occurred, you can generally forget about conception control and fear of pregnancy. Women virtually never conceive more than two years after the last menstrual period. Even six months generally proves that all chance of pregnancy has passed in a woman whose cycle remained regular throughout. To put your fears definitely at rest, however, there's nothing like an authoritative pronouncement by your own physician after a complete examination. Perhaps you will not want to have an examination especially for this purpose, but you can certainly make it a point to ask about your fertility the next time you visit your physician after an apparent menopause.

Fear of injury.

Most parents warn their little girls about the risk of self-injury, and quite often make their point in too strong and frightening a way. Early experiences in a doctor's office or with internal feminine hygiene products tend to make a woman expect discomfort whenever her husband makes the least error in sexual practice. Husbands often share this paralyzing idea. Even self-manipulations required for birth control practice (as when inserting a diaphragm) may evoke considerable fear and dread, creating a poor atmosphere for relaxed sexual communion.

Both husband and wife should carefully keep from giving any basis for injury fears, especially in relation to the sex act itself. The measures discussed in previous chapters to ensure a bride's comfortable introduction to sex help a great deal. Carefully trimmed fingernails and adequate use of either natural or artificial lubricants in *every* sex episode also prevent discomforts. Positions involving deep sexual penetration call for some special precautions, too: wait until several weeks of sexual adjustment have stretched the female organ thoroughly before attempting the harsher postures like the wife-astride and wife's-heels-on-husband's-shoulders positions, and always be certain that preliminary play has relaxed the vagina completely before going to maximum depth in these positions.

A frank discussion of the female organ's liability to injury often helps to resolve unreasonable fears. Given trimmed nails, a few weeks of adaptation and adequate preliminary play to assure lubrication and relaxation, a man can carry out almost any caress or sexual maneuver with absolutely no chance of doing his wife any injury. The twinges of pain which occasionally result in positions involving deep penetration signify stretching or pinching of highly sensitive organs, and do not result in injury. In fact, sexual injury *never* occurs in well established marriage, since the female organs become sufficiently stretched and relaxed to accommodate the male without injury even without adequate preparation after a time, and even the most brutal husband would not continue in the face of such intense and painful vaginal spasm as would be required to make possible any lasting damage. Feminine self-injury also never occurs if you observe a few simple precautions. Trimmed nails,

proper technique for inserting a diaphragm if you
decide to use one, and proper lubrication for self-
manipulations generally remove all risks and set your
mind thoroughly at rest.

Fear of failure or inadequacy.

The marriage bed makes a very poor proving
ground for either a man or a woman. In fact, the
whole orientation toward *individual* capabilities instead of *couple* success leads to many extra strains and
disappointments. If you blame yourself for sexual inadequacies, the resulting lack of self-confidence makes
your problem worse. If you blame your partner, the
resulting couple frictions and the effects on your partner's confidence take their toll. But if you view the
situation *constructively as a couple,* you can make a
great deal of progress without the paralyzing emotional elements of guilt or blame.

Successful couple adjustment virtually never involves consistently mutual orgasm. If you pursue this
goal, you will be disappointed. Dr. Kinsey's studies
showed that the best matched couples regard mutual
orgasm on about two-fifths of sexual occasions as par.
Many well-satisfied couples achieve it much more
rarely than that. Moreover, these ratios become established only after complete sexual adjustment. A
woman who experiences orgasm in the first few weeks
of marriage can count herself fortunate indeed, with
one to five years the usual interval for full sexual
awakening.

Most brides and grooms have been stuffed full of
romantic nonsense about the delights of the honeymoon. They therefore become convinced that either
they or their partners are sexual cripples long before

full response is even possible, and spend the rest of their married lives under a pall of self-recrimination and doubt. The early "failures," which should have been taken as a matter of course, become rankling sources of guilt and sexual inferiority, and themselves paralyze any efforts at improvement.

Sound sexual success, which leaves both parties always free of sexual discontent and brings substantial gratifications from sex to both, sometimes involves no wifely orgasms at all. Certainly, your aim should be couple adjustment rather than proved individual prowess. Freed of the pressure to prove male potency by sustained intercourse and to prove feminine responsiveness by orgastic joys, many couples find that they can relax into exactly the type of success they previously remained too upset ever to enjoy.

One last point: even though sexual success or failure in the long run is a couple responsibility, you can help to build your partner's confidence and contribute substantially to ultimate couple success by praising or acknowledging his or her sexual achievements. You don't have to force such comments, so long as you make them whenever they apply. "You were terrific tonight!" "What a woman!" or a dozen other remarks which give credit where credit is due cost very little effort, and genuinely help your sex life over a period of time.

Guilt from over-restrictive early training.

Your parents probably taught you that sex had no place in your life until you were ready for a mature and considered alliance. However, they probably put more emphasis on the *unsuitability* of sex before you form such a mature alliance than on its *suitability* and *unrestricted propriety* afterward. From a practical standpoint, they were probably right. A parent has to tell his schoolboy son that it is wrong to take down little girls' panties even though he knows that he will never explain with equal emphasis that such intimacies are all right in marriage. A parent has to make his little girl afraid of sexual advances by strange men, even if he cannot possibly give equal and simultaneous emphasis to the importance of *not* being afraid on the honeymoon. Although you might be able to balance these factors better for the next generation, you really can't blame your parents for leaving you plagued with sexual inhibitions. Without those inhibitions, you might have been married in haste at a tender age indeed.

You can take several important steps against sexual inhibitions. You can recognize their existence, their harmfulness in marriage and their irrationality.

A diary which includes your recollections of early and persisting inhibitions, false modesty, embarrassments, evidences of awareness of sex in others and in yourself often helps. After writing down all the significant experiences you recall, go back over the list and ask yourself questions like these:

"How did this shape my moral sense about sex?"

"Does the lesson I learned that day really apply to sex in marriage, or only to childhood experiments?"

"Were the attitudes which others revealed (and which I may have absorbed to some extent) really correct, and do they apply to *all* sexual experience or only to sex experience outside marriage?"

The answers to these questions often reveal an unsound basis for paralyzing or inhibiting ideas. Bringing such facts out in the open may prove very helpful indeed. For instance, one young man told me of hiding himself from the other boys at military school while in his teens. A young lady of eighteen feared pregnancy after her beau had done nothing more than kiss her. Both enjoyed notable improvement in sexual adjustment after discussing the origins of such misinformation-based behavior.

Unduly constraining sexual modesty.

A number of couples have difficulty with satisfaction-wrecking tensions unless they have total privacy for both advanced preliminaries and for intercourse itself. Some men and women even find the presence of a new-born infant disturbing. An exaggerated need for privacy may show up in connection with morning and daytime episodes, or in poor sexual response whenever any light filters through to the bedroom. Some couples find that older children or adults in range of hearing disturb their aplomb even if nobody can possibly see them. The presence of specific individuals may prove disturbing when nobody else makes any difference: several couples have told me that they have never achieved sexual success when in the same home with the wife's parents, for instance.

If you find yourself plagued by extra privacy needs, you usually can manage quite well by simply providing the right kind of occasions. Timing your encounters to be sure the children are sound asleep, arranging your rooms to provide proper concealment, or even simply closing the bedroom door may provide the extra privacy you need. If difficulties attach to the presence of certain people in the home, you can choose between conceding to this problem or attempting to uproot it through psychological counseling. Usually you will find it easier to keep a separate household than to review the background of your sexual attitudes in great detail. If sex always proves much more satisfying when you get away from home, you might consider absolute privacy as a necessary part of the framework for sex in your particular case, and try to provide this need in your household if possible.

Transferred taboos and upsets.

Most emotional relationships in maturity develop from models which date back to childhood. Your first attraction to your spouse might trace from some resemblance to your parent or your sister, for instance. Even though the relationship later becomes quite individual, some trace of this origin by transference—by applying feelings to this new object which you first developed toward another—still remains. Thus sexual advances and attentions which would have been improper with the original figure may carry guilt because of the transference. Levels of intimacy which may have been unwelcome from the original figure become repugnant. The barriers to incest rear up between you and your somewhat mother-like or father-like spouse.

These problems usually solve themselves as your relationship grows. However, you can help your spouse to achieve a separate image of you in several ways. Try to please him in your own way instead of falling into the family patterns. Cook your own way instead of getting his mother's recipes, for instance. Work out your own approach to splitting family chores instead of falling into the one your wife's family has used. Set styling of your hair, clothing and so on to emphasize differences instead of similarities between yourself and close family figures.

Sources of aid and counseling.

Discussions of the emotional interconnections between members of your own household, your parents and your in-laws often become quite sticky. Early attitude-forming experiences may not come out readily in ordinary conversation. Both in avoiding further upheaval and in getting to pay dirt fast, a trained counselor can often help you. If you feel that emotional associations and constraints have created a real problem in your home, a trip to a marriage counselor's office probably will straighten out the difficulties much more quickly than anything you can manage on your own. Your minister, priest or rabbi, social workers in the nearest Family Service Agency, or perhaps your family doctor (if you have an unusually understanding one) can give help if professional marriage counseling is not readily available. Some trained school counselors, especially at the high school level, spend enough time in the family relations area to be helpful also. Avoid sex quacks, though—let your doctor or someone else who knows the field recommend a qualified counselor instead of choosing one out of the telephone book.

How to put this chapter's advice to work for you.

Emotional constraints hamper almost every couple in their pursuit of sexual success. Whether such difficulties have led to notable problems or not, you will probably profit from giving attention to them.

Even women who *want* a baby suppress rather than rid themselves of the natural pregnancy fear. You can deal with that fear more easily if you acknowledge its existence without recrimination. Frank couple discussion of family plans also helps. If you decide on birth control, choice of method depends somewhat on your religious convictions. Rhythm control is available to virtually everyone. If you confine sexual relations to the period before Day Nine or the period after Day Nineteen with an average cycle, pregnancy becomes much less frequent. Corrections for a short or long cycle and zeroing in with basal temperature studies increase the effectiveness of period control somewhat. If you feel free to use chemical and mechanical agents, the diaphragm method makes the best starting point, suppositories or jellies often interfere the least with sex gratification after the first few months of marriage, and rubbers sometimes have a place (although seldom as the principal means of control). Combinations of methods reduce likelihood of pregnancy somewhat and improve the wife's confidence. In some instances, especially after failure of one accepted birth control method, the assurance gained makes the ritual and clutter worthwhile. Whether you use birth control or not, an occasional frank discussion of what you will do if a pregnancy develops helps to hold down pregnancy fears. A doctor's pronouncement that fertility has ceased makes the menopause more effective release from pregnancy fears.

You can quell fear of sexual injury, which generally stems from childhood warnings and early experiences, by comfortable introduction to sex, trimmed nails, adequate lubrication and so on. After the honeymoon, you will find it virtually impossible to injure the female organs with sexual activity. Frank discussion of that fact often helps.

Probably the best antidote to fear of sexual failure or inadequacy is the couple viewpoint espoused throughout this book. Work together toward a reasonable goal of sexual success and you will never have to apply terms like "frigid" or "impotent" to either yourself or your partner. The vicious circle of anxiety over "inadequacy" leading to further failures and further anxieties constitutes one of the biggest plagues to marriage. Dodge this difficulty by sticking to *couple* attack on *couple* goals, forgetting the whole false notion that one or the other of you must be at fault.

Guilty constraint in sex stems mainly from "don't do it" instead of "wait until you're married" training in childhood. An autobiography with regard to sexual attitudes, modesty, sources of knowledge and so on may help to crystallize restrictions which no longer apply, and may rid your marriage of troublesome restraints. In some cases, social attitudes toward incest or early conflict with parental figures contribute to sexual restraint. These problems usually solve themselves as your individual relationship develops. You can help by making your marriage independent of your spouse's family pattern, and by never playing upon any resemblance you have to his family members.

If simple measures leave substantial unsolved problems or persistent constraint, a trained counselor can often give highly worthwhile assistance.

8.
How to Build
a Domestic Framework
for Sublime Sex

Trying to put together a mutually satisfying sexual episode during domestic upheaval is like trying to roll a cigarette on the back of a runaway horse. Any emotional disturbance affects your sex life. Disturbances in your man-woman relationship breed especially troublesome conflicts and anxieties. Ordinary business or household worries distract you from passion-building dalliance and caress. Such problems wreak havoc upon connubial bliss.

On the other hand, deliberate efforts to free each other of emotional burdens and to improve each other's mood often pay off in exceedingly pleasant sexual communion. Deliberate efforts to set up varied occasions for relaxed, unhurried intercourse and to set up emotionally pleasant linkages with sexual activity make a big difference, too. Deliberate efforts to improve the quality of your personal relationship through the years reflect themselves in improved sexual harmony as well as in general household peace.

Easing troubled minds before sex.

When your partner seems preoccupied, tense or

moody, sexual communion usually remains below par until he or she gets straightened out. Many couples make the mistake of trying to cheer each other up *with* sex instead of cheering each other up *for* it. Sex is a fair weather friend, delightful in good times but grudging and niggardly with its rewards when circumstances get you down.

Sometimes, you can help your partner pull out of a bad mood or shed excess tensions by helping with a troublesome situation. Everything from the household budget to better discipline for youngsters might be involved here, so details go far beyond the scope of this book. However, if *sex* yields less than you have reason to expect, one of your first steps should be to see whether *life* is yielding all that you and your partner might expect, and what you can do to make things better.

It often helps to discuss the situations which bother you or your partner, even if you cannot change them in any way. Each of you airs his feelings through discussion. Each of you crystallizes his own thoughts as well as getting the other's advice. In fact, the key role in soothing tensions and helping with problems is often that of the sympathetic listener—patient, willing to stand behind the troubled individual in any course he decides upon, helpful in suggesting possible solutions or sources of aid, but never presuming to take over the other person's rightful responsibilities.

Even if you cannot help your partner to resolve problems and concerns permanently, you can often get his mind off them before a sexual encounter. An entertaining evening or a companionable chat before bedtime sets the stage for relaxed consummation. If you enjoy and approve of alcoholic beverages, a highball often proves relaxing (although not enough so to make me recommend one unless it fits in with your usual customs). Heavy alcoholic indulgence generally impairs sexual capacities to some degree even when it promotes the urge, and seems unwise.

A few of my patients find that mild tranquilizers or mood-lifting stimulants help them toward sexual success. The effect never justifies use of these agents in relaxed and cheerful people. However, sexual impairment is frequently one of the first and most disturbing effects of tension or depression, so that medications to correct such states may prove worthwhile as aids to sexual success when other disturbances of function would not make you want medication.

Reminders of past glories.

When the Russian scientist, Dr. Ivan Pavlov, fed dogs immediately after ringing a certain bell, he soon found that ringing the bell would make the dogs' mouths water even when no food was on the way. In the same way, repeated sexual encounter between husband and wife leads each to associate certain sights, sounds, smells and other sensory premonitors of union with impending bliss. Properly managed, the conditioning of sexual response can actually increase sexual arousal and enjoyment far beyond what either of you could expect through relationship with a variety of partners.

If you want certain elements of your appearance, dress or manner to reinforce your sex appeal with recollection of past delights, you must obviously reserve those elements for occasions when sexual delights seem definitely in the offing. A certain degree of modesty has some place in marriage for this reason. A wife who ordinarily keeps her more intimate parts concealed from her husband's wandering eye can arouse him mightily by baring her breast or letting her robe fall away from her naked thigh. Such glimpses soon come to mean as much to him as an ardent caress —his subconscious mind signals that they mean sexual joy, just as the tinkling bell signaled Pavlov's dogs that food was on the way. But what if she bares her whole body to him morning and night in matter-of-fact disrobement? Will her smooth breast still stir his passion after he has watched her dress a dozen times when sexual encounter was remote? Even though you might not think it sensible to dress behind a screen when every inch of your anatomy is thoroughly familiar to your mate, free display of absolute nudity as an everyday event robs you of an otherwise effective means of arousing his ardor.

Certain caresses likewise keep their significance best if used when sex looms incarnate. For instance, one of my patients once complained that he could hardly find a way to stir his wife's passion any more. Early in marriage, he had fallen into the habit of sleeping with one hand on his wife's breast and the other resting on her genitals. His goodnight routine when he had no thought of sex involved a thorough exploration of her physical delights which could only be likened to a covetous miser taking inventory. After being pawed over nightly and held constantly in intimate embrace, no wonder the lady became a bit hard to arouse! It took almost a year of twin-bed living to make his advances seem significant again.

Not that twin beds work out best in most marriages: you can probably keep your caresses from getting stale by exercising a little self-control without such measures. Simply distinguish in your own mind between caresses which you want to reserve for passion-inflaming purposes and those which seem proper to casual demonstration of affection. As a rule of thumb, you might try reserving for times when sex seems in the offing all intimacies which you consider improper in the presence of other members of your family.

Besides reserving certain forms of enticement and caress for definitely sex-associated occasions, you can get considerable passion-generating help from smells, sounds and other sensations which have been deliberately or accidentally associated with sexual fruition. Natural body odors stemming from the fluids poured out by glands in the vagina and from slight changes in the odor of sweat and breath (not from simple lack of cleanliness, which usually kills passion instead of generating it) serve this purpose for some couples, so that you need not feel embarrassed if you become conscious of such odors before, during or after sexual encounter. You can link a certain odor with sexual excitement by applying scented preparations beforehand whenever your partner's behavior tells you that intercourse will probably occur. Women can use perfume or cologne for this purpose, while men usually choose a scented grooming aid such as hair dressing or aftershave lotion. Some couples link the aroma of an open fire, scent sprayed into the air or a mildly pervasive incense with sexual communion. The sense of taste can implement sexual arousal, especially if you feed each other sweetmeats and special treats as part of your love play. Some couples link certain liqueurs or wines with sexual preliminaries. Soft music in the background means more and more as sexual successes compound its significance. Certain negligees, reserved for occasions of special ardor, take on extra exciting qualities.

You cannot use all of these modes of conditioning

to build each other's excitement, but you can almost certainly pick two or three practical techniques to use reasonably often. The trick is to anticipate when the *other person* will almost certainly experience sexual delights, then provide certain smells, sights, sounds or other sensations to link this episode with others in the past and future. Whenever you predict your partner's coming satisfaction from preliminary caresses and evident good mood or from your own responsive sexual desire, add a pleasant scent to your bedtime toilet, don a special garment or provide a bedtime refreshment of a certain, significant type. Ultimately, this practice helps heighten new sexual encounters with memories of earlier bliss.

How to build a sounder personal relationship in marriage.

Physical pressures, frictions and stimulations alone can never bring you full sexual delight. You express your feeling for the other person in every sexual advance or submission. What you express adds greatly to his satisfaction, and what he expresses adds greatly to yours.

Although some people achieve or even prefer sex without deep, lasting, personal attachment, some form of personal relationship is indispensable. A man reared to hate womankind might get more satisfaction out of rape than from connubial union, and a woman who has never achieved lasting human ties might become sufficiently emotional about mere masculine interest to give adequate response, but the emotional element in these instances is warped, not totally missing.

If you can build close emotional bonds through which each of you responds quite keenly to the other's ardor and desire, connubial bliss improves. Conversely, if you find annoyance, resentment or doubt pervading your relationship, your sex life is usually disturbed.

Considerateness certainly helps. If you keep in mind the burdens which life in general, and your own needs and demands in particular, place upon your marriage partner, you will often find ways to help. Even if you cannot do anything about your partner's problems, you can ease his burdens through commiseration. Sharing burdens and commiserating in the face of difficulties definitely increase your capacity for sharing passionate excitement and building spirals of echoed and re-echoed sexual delight.

Although life affords you many opportunities to work together or commiserate with each other in meeting externally caused problems, it also involves many conflicts of interest inside the team. The good American life abounds in choices on which a man and wife can disagree, ranging from selecting one TV show over another to residing in your home town or pursuing greater business opportunity elsewhere. No single formula solves these problems: The idea of "fifty-fifty" merely focuses your attentions on coming out even and multiplies arguments instead of preventing them, for instance. You have to go more than half way in marriage to come out with good teamwork. You have to put the other person's welfare and happiness on a par with your own in all of your acts and decisions, and give in or fail to give in (which can sometimes be even more difficult) according to the welfare of the team instead of your immediate desires.

Most couples freely admit the necessity for following this course. Even husbands and wives who have brought their marriage to the verge of collapse through petty conflicts tell a marriage counselor that the whole batch of issues over which they fight makes less difference to them than the marriage itself. Most people would gladly sacrifice the *issues* and even many *principles* to keep their marital relationship sound, but they cannot sacrifice their *feeling of personal worth* or their *self-concept* as the required concessions demand. Your mind keeps you from recognizing the ways in which you shield these two crucial qualities from bruising or upset, but it does not keep you from using awareness of this basic problem in two different ways to strengthen your marriage:

1. *You can help your partner to feel worthwhile as a person through ordinary compliments.*

Whatever you can compliment about your partner's appearance, character or behavior certainly deserves remark. You will find that many perfectly proper occasions for such comment arise without resorting to lies or exaggeration. Too many husbands and wives take each other's good points for granted and never express appreciation of them. A few words of genuine, heartfelt praise or thanks often do a great deal of good. In particular, you should remark praiseworthy points connected with areas in which feelings of inadequacy often strike. For wives, such areas include attractiveness, sexual competence, soundness in child-rearing effort and ability as a homemaker. For husbands, they might be masculine adequacy, command of community and family respect.

Perhaps the greatest compliment is confident assignment of responsibility. A husband whose wife leaves him the reins of sexual communion feels considerable buoying of his self-esteem. Likewise the wife whose husband says, "You're doing fine" and leaves her a free hand in managing her household.

2. *You can avoid challenges to your partner's self-concept by meeting his or her need for concerned support without disturbing self-sufficiency.*

In marriage, you need to balance self-reliance on the one hand against genuine concern for your partner and genuine need for loving emotional support. You need to feel capable of standing on your own two feet. You also need to depend upon your partner—to yearn for and receive evidence of his concern and interest.

You can both develop such two-way support without losing control of your individual destinies or confidence in your individual powers through *compassion:* emotional sharing of each other's trials. You can feel for your partner and let your partner know that you are behind him without taking over decisions which are rightfully his and without attempting to change attitudes and convictions essential to his integrity. In other words, you can give your husband or wife helpful support without dominating him, undermining his confidence or disturbing his integrity.

Besides respect for your husband or wife as a person, this principle presupposes some division of responsibility (such as the classic wage earner-homemaker one) and a way to settle issues encountered in areas of joint responsibility. You will find helpful material on these points in the books on marriage and family living mentioned in the preface to this book; or you can seek counsel from your religious adviser, Family Service Agency, marriage counselor or physician.

How to build emotional closeness in marriage.

A close relationship lets you share another person's feelings quite intensely. In sexual communion, this sharing leads to a delightful spiral. Your passion begets excitement in your partner, which in turn builds passion further. Such echoing of feelings also builds the relationship itself: if you share many emotionally significant experiences, your lives blend more and more into a welded whole in which what happens to your partner stirs you just as much as what happens to you personally.

Shared activities help to build such unity of feeling. If you reveal your feelings freely to each other in all sorts of experiences, you draw steadily closer to each other. Shared interests thus help to build the climate in which spirals of feeling can flourish, and definitely improve your sex life as well as married life in general.

The closest form of personal relationship goes beyond shared feeling to shared pride. If you gain self-esteem from your partner's accomplishments (or shame in his discomfiture) equivalent to what you would feel if you were in his place, you have reached the point of merged identities. Most couples do not live constantly at this plane. Over the breakfast table, they function as mere friends no matter how close they can get to one another in times of crisis or intimate exchange. In moments of closeness, however, you can build this feeling by carefully approaching every issue as a team instead of as competitors. Problems of sex and family life particularly deserve this viewpoint, with which the ritual union of sex and the merged identities of reproduction conform perfectly. This is one more strong reason for learning sexual techniques together as a couple instead of independently. In the intimacy of the marriage bed, you can build emotional union through which all of life's joys can multiply and all its burdens greatly diminish: but these advantages follow only if you work *together* toward a sound sex life, not if you each attempt to acquire specific masculine or feminine skill.

How to put this chapter's main points to work for you.

Sexual satisfaction stems from emotional interplay which occurs more freely when both partners feel content with life and with each other. You should try to cheer up your partner *before* sexual relations instead of depending on sex to solve mood problems. Do what you can to make his or her life happier. Learn to give comfort when you cannot give aid. Try to improve his mood temporarily with recreation or pleasant distraction. Ask your doctor about tranquilizers if need be.

You can probably build sexual excitement more readily in future episodes if you link your sexual successes with certain scents or garments. A degree of modesty and reserve in using intimate caress helps you to make your attentions more exciting through the years instead of letting them lose significance. Scented grooming aids, certain negligees, bedtime refreshments and other means of linking smells, tastes and sensations with sexual enticement also help. Settle on one or two such stimulations and apply them whenever you expect your partner to get great satisfaction in a sexual encounter. You will soon find that the stimulus itself rouses his passion by recalling these past glories.

A good personal relationship helps you to excite

and respond to each other. Considerateness and compassionate commiseration in everyday life reflect themselves in your sex life as well as elsewhere. Differences of opinion and conflicts of interest cause less strain if you do not allow them to interfere with either party's feeling of worth or self-concept. Building the other person's self-assurance through complimenting any deserving quality or act and giving emotional support in ways which do not challenge the other person's authority or integrity also help. Shared interests and activities with free expression of all emotions and feelings builds the kind of closeness through which sexual excitement burgeons. A shared attack on sexual problems and sexual ignorance is especially important.

9.
How to Generate
Feminine Fervor

As a couple, you cannot always wait for passionate feminine desire before proceeding with sexual intercourse. In order to build a sound sex life together, you must satisfy the husband's needs from the very start, and in the process develop the wife's erotic nature. Relaxed and willing service to a loved and loving husband provides a wife with steadily deepening emotional satisfaction—satisfaction which ultimately burgeons into anticipatory passion, keen sexual excitement and the intense reward of orgasm. This build-up of sexual desire and excitability takes time, and also requires exposure in the sexual situation. A wife cannot conquer sexual constraint or develop ardent desire by hanging back until the spirit moves her, or by lying in passive immobility and trying to think of something else while her husband takes care of his sexual needs. She almost always has to develop her ability to please and begin to take definite pride in that capacity before the full flower of feminine arousal blooms in her breast. In fact, women who find themselves hard to arouse almost always must school themselves to carry out the sex act deliberately, pro-

ficiently and consistently upon request before they
have much chance of frequent orgastic reward.

Both the hard-to-arouse wife and her husband
should recognize the fact that willing sexual indulgence almost always has to precede passionate sexual
response. The husband should not hang back from
sexual activity simply because his wife cannot respond
with heartfelt, involuntary ardor. He should be considerate in his demands, of course, to the extent that
he curbs sex urges which arise at markedly inconven-
ient times. Even the wife who almost always enjoys an
orgasm during sexual episodes resents advances while
she is dressing to go to a party or in the middle of
cooking a meal. But he should not restrain his passion
for days on end in the hope of finding his wife in a
responsive mood or let the fatigue which his wife
suffers from the ordinary burdens and tensions of an
ordinary day discourage his advances. Basically, his
passion is the spark which must ultimately kindle hers.
In indulging his desires and sharing his feelings
through the emotional echoing of true love, his wife
will grow in ardor. He does neither his wife nor himself any good by sharply decreasing the number of
sexual episodes or by restraining his passions until
they become conflict-ridden and dulled. Especially, he
harms couple sex life by restraint which leaves him
fighting the hair-trigger urgency of pent-up desire
when his wife finally does show signs of response: to
leave her hanging without satisfaction at this point
destroys an opportunity for passionate awakening
which might take months to reconstruct.

On the other hand, excessive sexual stimulation of
an unaroused woman accomplishes nothing. When the
wife indulges her husband for the sake of couple
harmony and of ultimate success, violent sex-mimick-

ing caresses will not arouse her passion. The husband should follow his sexual urges without too much concern for feminine pace on such occasions, so long as he takes time and precautions to assure his wife's comfort. Her reward on these occasions is the echoing of his pleasure, to which prolonged caressing of the female organ contributes very little. When it seems clear that feminine passion simply cannot come, the husband need feel no guilt or anxiety and should avoid frantic attempts to remedy the situation. Instead, he should relax and enjoy the benefits his wife confers on him in the firm knowledge that this is the best thing he can do to help the couple toward ultimate sexual success.

In some instances, you will both realize from the start that wifely ardor has not been aroused and can modify your sexual approach accordingly. Soft kisses and stroking caresses generally prove quite suitable, but light bodily caresses usually tickle and annoy her when she serves her husband's needs instead of her own passions. Relatively firm, matter-of-fact enjoyment of her pleasure-giving parts fits such occasions better than hesitant or tantalizing brushes or silky caress. While the man's attentions should never be rough, they should be forthright and tenderly possessive instead of hesitant and namby-pamby.

If the least glimmer of passionate response develops, you may want to follow the first wave of sex play with an interval of quiet companionship in the hope that further response will come when you renew advances. However, if you get no emotional response during intimate sex play, you probably will gain little or nothing by prolonged preliminaries. Perhaps the best index of passion is the moistness of the female opening: if you arrive at the point of genital caress and find the tissues quite slick with natural lubrication and reasonably well relaxed, whisper to your wife: "Keep me going for a little while and I'll try to bring you along." If you find the tissues rather dry and tight, you will not get your wife to the point of orgasm no matter what you do. Gentle caresses to spur formation of some fluid and to transfer it from vagina to inner lips and clitoris may aid her comfort, or artificial lubrication may be wise. But heavy sexual stimulation only adds to the woman's burden without bringing her any joy.

When you commence sex contact with an unimpassioned partner, always linger at the outer surface for a while. A woman with emotional blocks against feminine fervor (whether from over-prim rearing, associated fears or conflicts) often tightens up the moment her husband assumes the sex posture. He might find the vagina fairly well relaxed in preliminary play and still find it too tight to admit one finger when he is ready to make entrance. By shifting position so that the penis rubs along the female opening instead of jabbing into it, approaching almost directly from above instead of from down between your partner's legs, you can continue pleasurable and exciting frictions for yourself without causing uncomfortable ones for your wife. The vagina usually loosens up in a short time, allowing the head of the penis to enter freely. You can then combine short in and out motions (keeping to the outer inch or so of the vagina) with surface frictions until relaxation becomes complete. Intercourse in the usual manner proves entirely comfortable for both partners thereafter.

Most women have intervals when they are hard to arouse even after full sexual awakening. A couple often remains in some doubt as to their chance for

mutual orgasm until sex play has already gone quite
far. To add to the confusion, many actually unin-
spired wives play the part of passion in an effort to
please their mates. Actually, no great harm results if
you misread the signals occasionally so long as the
vagina is moist and relatively relaxed. However,
couples who try it both ways usually find that a wife
can please her husband more, enjoy her feminine role
more, and cement the emotional bonds of matrimony
just as thoroughly by frankly serving her husband's
needs as by pretense. The man who knows that only
his own pace counts gets more pleasure from the
episode than he would achieve by matching his wife's
apparent rhythm. Deliberately exciting feminine
caresses bring a husband to just as great a height as
falsely passionate ones. While the emotional echoing
of a mutually passionate encounter builds higher than
any deliberate maneuver and the delights of mutual
orgasm reign supreme, frank sexual technique still
makes a better substitute than false squeals of feminine delight. Perhaps a few men need the fiction of
passionate response to convince them of their own
sexual worth, but most accept their wives' willingness
to be possessed as equally valid evidence of marital
success.

Prompt repetition.

Some women never reach an orgasm because their
sexual nature demands several progressively higher
waves of excitement before the ultimate peak. Their
husbands lead them to the foothills, carefully coordinate the male climax with a modest height, and
then retreat before they reach the snow-capped moun-
tains. Even a husband with vast sexual capability

often lets this situation persist for many years by constantly laying off after each less-than-satisfying event and making only as much sexual contact as his nature absolutely demands. Men with slower rhythm almost never hit upon the rapid-fire combination which wakens wifely response unless they do so in deliberate campaigns.

If female orgasm rarely rewards your sexual efforts even after an adequate period for awakening of wifely zeal, three steps will help you to find out if you are quitting on preliminary peaks, and will simultaneously solve the problem:

1. *Play past two or three surges of feminine feeling.*
Start sexual dalliance while still dressed, play past a surge of female feeling, then break for a cigarette, a quiet conversation, a few dances to the radio or some other intimate but not directly sexual interval. Resume sex play when the spirit moves you, and play through another feminine climax. Linger in each other's arms this time, and rebuild fervor as soon as feminine desire shows in the wife's caresses or response. Play all three or four preliminary peaks or even orgasms at increasing pace before attempting intercourse.

2. *Concentrate encounters into a short period.*
Some women need the stimulation of actual sex contact to get them past each preliminary peak, and then need further sexual encounter almost during the afterglow to reach their final climax. With fast-paced couples, this might mean two or three repetitions in one night. Others do best by concentrating several episodes during one week (usually just at the end of menstruation, both because the menstrual holiday which most couples observe makes the occa-

sion ripe and because many women prove most responsive then) rather than spacing out encounters through the woman-month.

3. *Build up to climactic sex with several preliminary episodes.*

A few couples find that each climactic episode ends a three- or four-day campaign of occasional nonclimactic sexual contact. You should try out this pattern if male sex rhythm will not otherwise permit a concentration of three or four episodes into one weekend. Make sexual contact Saturday morning and take lots of time for relaxed dalliance. Let the urge settle itself slowly, then break for your morning meal. Build a surge of sex excitement later in the day or evening, and again prolong sex contact for as long as possible without going into climactic activity. Usually you will find that a slowly aroused woman settles back down slowly, too. Each new encounter's excitement builds on residuals from the previous one. By the third or fourth encounter, you can often reach a keenly mutual climax with no strain at all.

Concern about imagined sexual inadequacy.

A great many couples who worry about "frigidity" simply expect the ultimate in sexual rewards too quickly. When the woman does not have an orgasm by the end of her honeymoon, she begins to wonder whether something is wrong with her sexual nature. Anxiety tinges every sexual incident from then on. She tries so hard to work herself up that she quenches any spark of ardor at its start. Sometimes sexual awakening finally occurs, but lingering doubts and fears still decrease the full flower of her response.

Even after complete sexual awakening, however, a woman often finds that nothing which her husband can do will arouse her ardor. Here again, inflated expectations often cause undue concern. A few incidents when the wife's enjoyment stems mainly from echoing of her husband's pleasure and pride in her ability to please remain part of most marriages for life.

Patient expectation and a slight scaling down of goals often relieve you of emotional burdens which play a big part in impending feminine response. Have faith in your capacity to respond, in your husband's capacity to satisfy you, and in the depth of your affection. A few sexual failures should not cast doubt on any of these things or cloud your sexual outlook with anxiety and fear. Simply follow the step by step program for sexual adjustment or rehabilitation reviewed in the final chapter of this book and your passionate nature will almost certainly make itself known.

Sex-related injury, self-injury and injury fear.

As small children, most women receive frightening advice to "keep your hands off that area down there or you might hurt yourself." Later on, teachers and parents often plant the idea that slight pressures or injuries can do permanent damage to the female organ. While most such injunctions aim at preserving the virginal membrane, which ceases to be a valid concern after marriage, the general prohibitions leave many women with an exaggerated fear of anything which might conceivably do injury to their genitals and with an unduly great emotional response to any discomfort which might indicate such injury.

Probably the most common trigger for such fears

is fingernail friction. Women encounter the fingernail as an actual or potential injury agent in three common ways, all of which can attach passion-quenching fear to the sex act in the sensitive minds:

¶ First, painful twinges or later irritation stemming from the husband's jagged or untrimmed nails often pull passion up short during the latter stages of sex play. Each such episode leaves some legacy of fear which impairs future response. The impaired response cuts down natural lubrication so that fingernail scratching and other discomforts during sex play or intercourse become more likely. I have seen several women whose sex life was unsatisfactory for a period of years on this basis. Fortunately, a few weeks of sex contact carefully conducted to eliminate all possibility of discomfort or injury (with special emphasis on the husband's nails) interrupts this vicious circle with excellent results.

¶ Second, the fear of self-injury while inserting a diaphragm or carrying out other birth control procedures links paralyzing emotional upset to later sexual activity in some women's minds. A generation ago, many people believed that serious self-injury or loss of the virginal membrane (which was still commonly used as the only definite evidence of purity) might follow self-manipulation. Holding this belief, it was only right that they teach their children a hands-off policy. Since their own knowledge was somewhat hazy, the explanations they gave tended to be vague and frightening. Although everybody talks much more freely about sex facts today, I still find a good many patients deeply imbued with the idea that it is morally wrong and medically dangerous to insert a finger into the vagina to check the position of a diaphragm. Add to this lingering vestige of an outmoded sexual code the frightening image of a sharp, long fingernail and you often get a burden of fear which casts a pall over the whole of a woman's sex life.

¶ Last, a few of my patients have been so thoroughly imbued in childhood with fear of self-injury that even the manipulation needed for use of internally worn pads during menstruation causes paralyzing fear. This fear generally has concentrated upon the fingernails. Trimming the nails or using a rubber glove during insertion usually gives relief.

Next to fingernail injury, stretching of delicate female tissues by poorly lubricated sexual frictions probably bestirs the greatest fear of genital injury. While fully aroused feminine ardor usually makes the vagina quite moist with natural lubricants, the wife who accommodates her husband more in loving service than in passion usually forms very little vaginal juice. In some cases, this dearth of lubrication leads to discomfort during intercourse, which in turn leads to passion-quenching fear in future encounters, more dearth of lubrication and so on through the barren, tension-ridden months.

When couples complain of lack of wifely passion, they almost always need some extra lubrication for a few weeks or months during sexual rehabilitation. Admittedly, too much lubrication may cut down the man's pleasure somewhat. However, it is better to err in this direction until the woman can relax in absolute certainty that she will not be hurt than to perpetuate her passion-quenching fears with continual twinges of friction-generated discomfort. If you do not use a diaphragm or a rubber for birth control, petroleum jelly provides good lubrication. Be sure to get the plain, unmedicated variety, since some people get a rash from the phenol or carbolic acid which medicated products contain. Petroleum jelly rots rubber, so that you should use a glycerin base product like K-Y Jelly for lubrication if you use either a diaphragm or rubber. Most couples leave the husband in charge of lubrication, both because he can easily judge the need for it during ordinary sex play and because he can apply lubricants easily to his erect organ. Petroleum jelly has enough body to stay on the penis if applied there, and thus has advantages if the male takes care of lubrication. However, women who apply petroleum jelly as a lubricant often fail to coat the inner lips adequately, and the material does not spread well. If the wife lubricates her own sex organs, a glycerin base jelly such as K-Y usually works best.

If lack of feminine passion has been a problem, you should probably use extra lubrication every time for the first few weeks of sexual rehabilitation. Later, somewhat decreased lubrication may work out well. The husband can rub petroleum jelly onto the head of the penis once a day to keep the skin soft, and omit lubrication specifically at the time of sex contact. He can give extra attention to the lubricating caresses described in Chapter Three by which he transfers any fluid available from the upper vagina to the female opening and inner lips where sexual frictions are strongest. If natural moistures do not make the surfaces completely slick before time to commence sex contact, he can linger in surface friction for a few minutes to allow extra flow from the lubricating glands. However, he should have lubricant within reach always during the early months, and use it freely if the membranes stay the least bit dry or if his wife gives any sign of genital discomfort.

How to identify and correct response-impairing physical disorders.

Quite a few women suffer impaired sexual response as a result of some readily correctable physical condition, error in self-care technique or breach in couple sex practices. If any of the common problems of this sort plague you, you can probably recognize and correct the situation.

Genital rawness.

When disease or disorder makes the inside surface of the female organ somewhat raw and irritable, the muscular wall of the vagina may tighten up painfully in response to sexual frictions even though the rawness is too mild to cause discomfort at other times. One or two such incidents spread a pall of fear over future sexual encounters, and sometimes kick off a vicious circle: fear and spasm, leading to painful intercourse, which causes still more fear and spasm, and so on.

You can probably steer clear of such difficulties by remaining alert for conditions which cause female organ irritation, getting prompt medical examination and care (which usually will clear up these conditions in a short time), and using special measures to keep sexual friction entirely comfortable for the woman in the meanwhile.

Rawness after childbirth.

The danger that sexual intercourse will convey germs up into the uterus and cause serious infection generally abates inside eight days. However, soreness where the vagina has been stretched or cut during childbirth usually remains considerable for at least three weeks and deserves some extra consideration for several months. Chapter Eleven gives detailed instructions for getting through this period. If you have already gotten into a vicious circle of discomfort leading to spasm and thus to further discomfort, fear and spasm, you can usually get back on a sound footing by using couple techniques aimed at comfortable release instead of maximum pleasure for a time. Lubricate well with Surfacaine ointment, keep sexual frictions relatively gentle, and stick to the positions described in Chapter Four as suitable to the new bride. After a few weeks devoted to completely comfortable sex contact, the emotional barriers to feminine ardor which a few painful experiences have erected will usually fall.

Vaginal infections and infestations.

Infection at the mouth of the womb usually causes excess mucus to drain out through the female opening and stain the panties or clothing. The infection seldom causes frankly painful spasms during intercourse, but may interfere somewhat with full feminine fervor. If you suspect such a condition, you should check with your doctor both to free yourself of the messiness and possible sexual effects of infection and to dispose of the cancer-spurring effect of lingering disease. (One study showed that a thousand women treated for such infections developed only two cancers of the mouth of the womb instead of the twenty-two which would otherwise have been expected, which means that one out of every fifty of them saved herself from a very serious state by having a few simple medical treatments.)

An irritating, frothy discharge which causes either itching or scalding of the female opening usually comes from *trichomonas*. *Trichomonas* are organisms much larger than ordinary germs, but not quite large enough to identify with the naked eye. Your doctor can easily find them by looking at a drop of fluid from the vagina through a microscope, and can usually cure the condition for you without painful or expensive maneuvers. Pain during intercourse frequently occurs in this condition, since the whole lining of the vagina is involved. A few women continue to get *trichomonas* trouble back again after seeming cure. If this happens to you, ask your husband to get an examination of his prostate gland, which may harbor a few organisms without causing him any complaints. Even though this condition usually spreads by non-sexual means and does not signify any sex contact outside of marriage, reseeding by an infected husband can occur. If you both get treatment at once, you usually stop having trouble.

One of the commonest conditions causing painful episodes during intercourse stems from pinworms. Over one-third of kindergarten-aged children have pinworms, and spread to other members of the family almost always occurs. The worms look like little bits of thread (although you will not ordinarily see them). They live up inside the intestine, but the female crawls out through the bowel opening at night to lay her eggs in the nearby folds of skin. In the adult, itching around the bowel and female openings which is especially bothersome at night suggests pinworms, especially if there are young children in the household. In the child, nightmares, whining and other signs of constant fatigue may be the only things you notice. If you look closely at the rectal area while the child is sleeping, perhaps at about eleven p.m., you may see the worms emerging to lay their eggs. A doctor can find worm eggs under the microscope by searching material taken from the skin surface near the rectum. Modern medicines cure pinworms quite readily and with little discomfort or upset.

Emotional tangles and feminine fervor.

A few women continue to find sexual relations uncomfortable, repugnant or unrewarding even after couple mastery of sexual technique and an adequate period of trial. Emotional tangles left over from childhood training, or early associations and experiences almost always prove to be at fault. Sometimes the measures advised in Chapter Seven help to assuage fears and guilts or get around passion-quenching emotional associations. Sometimes psychologic counseling by a psychiatrist, psychologist, professional marriage counselor, Family Service or parish social worker or religious adviser may prove helpful. Professional counseling almost always proves necessary when profound emotional reactions or marked physical manifestations of emotional upheaval (pounding heart, weak spells, nausea or the like) occur frequently in association with or in anticipation of sexual relations. Fortunately, however, measures aimed at the simple and readily correctable problems which this chapter discusses and the special techniques it outlines bring couples through to a successful sexual adjustment without prolonged counseling.

Relaxation and feminine fervor.

Besides relieving specific sexual fears and domestic pressures, you can often take specific action against passion-quenching tension either during or before a sexual encounter. Even if you know that tension stems from definite emotional difficulties, simple measures for relief often allow a good sexual adjustment and make professional counseling unnecessary. Moreover, sexual difficulties often stem from vicious circles of emotional constraint leading to sexual discomfort or failure which then leads to further constraint, and so on. You may be able to break up this pattern through special techniques or measures without attacking the emotional problem which originally started the snow-balling difficulties.

Stepwise relaxation.

When you loosen up muscles beyond the normal resting point by the deliberate stepwise technique discussed on pages 87-8, you definitely relieve passion-quenching tension. During early sex play, a degree of relaxation actually entices the husband with provocative languor even as it soothes the wife into receptive tranquility. Perhaps the husbands sits on the end of the davenport with his wife's head in his lap. Quiet music in the background and dim lights may prove suitable. The wife relaxes step by step in her husband's arms, using the technique described above. The first stirrings of passion will not prove too distracting. Even occasional languid response to the husband's caresses does not interrupt her program. She can generally dissipate most bodily tensions inside a few minutes without concentrating so intensely as to quell either her own or her husband's passion. Meanwhile, her husband lets his hands rove gently over her hair, her neck and her various bodily enticements. A soft kiss or an intimate caress occasionally tests her readiness for more intensive play: if she responds with ardor to the touch of his lips or catches her breath in impassioned sighs as his hand runs up her thigh, the interval of quiet play has served its purpose.

Special baths.

Some wives find that a tranquilizing tub bath before sexual encounter makes for relaxed responsiveness. This method takes forty-five minutes to an hour, so best get it out of the way while your husband is out bowling or is otherwise amused. Fill your tub with water at about 94 degrees. Tie a washcloth or towel to the faucet so that the water runs along it to allow noiseless flow. Get in the tub and roll another towel beneath your neck for relaxed comfort. Then adjust the taps to give a gentle flow of water slightly warmer than that already in the tub, so that the temperature stays constant in spite of natural cooling. Relax completely in the tub for at least three quarters of an hour and preferably longer. When your husband comes home or seems ready for bed, dress in a provocative negligee and join him in a relaxed and blissful sexual encounter.

Preliminary sleep.

Many wives who cannot respond well to their husbands' advances at the end of a hectic day find that they do much better after an interval of relaxing sleep. Sexual encounter in the relaxed torpor of early morning brings keenly mutual satisfaction to some couples. Others send the wife off to bed an hour or two before the husband, then rouse her from sound sleep for sexual dalliance. Occasionally, a high strung husband does better after preliminary sleep, too, so that some couples agree to wake each other whenever any impulse rouses them in the middle of the night.

If you use preliminary sleep for relaxation, be sure to take plenty of time for extra play. The party who wakes a sleeping mate usually has had a considerable period of anticipation in which to get excited. A husband is particularly likely to mistake the torpor of lingering sleep for acquiescent languor and proceed with intercourse too promptly. At least in early encounters, you should probably prepare a warm drink, tune in quiet music, and arouse your sleeping partner gently. After an interval of quiet companionship, your loving attentions will prove all the more welcome and the chance that you will misread the signals or proceed in spite of them much less.

Vacation for sex.

Sometimes you can give married sex a shot in the arm for months to come through a brief, second-honeymoon-type vacation. Young mothers find it particularly hard to relax for sexual dalliance at home, coming as they do directly from household chores to the marriage bed and never knowing when a crying child might interrupt connubial episodes. The restoration of satisfactory sex life after childbirth deserves full-time attention for a few days (after the baby has become reasonably self-sufficient) if you can possibly arrange it. A weekend in a downtown hotel, or even an evening which stretches far enough into the night for sexual encounter away from home, improves many women's responsiveness. A couple vacation helps your sex life much more than a family one as a rule, because the responsibilities of motherhood may involve considerable tension even when the physical burdens of home care have been relieved. If a better sex life seems crucial to your marriage, a few days spent exclusively on each other quite often prove worthwhile.

How to put this chapter's advice to work for you.

If difficulty in arousing feminine passion plagues your marriage, both of you should resign yourselves for a time to episodes in which active, willing wifely service meets the husband's passionate demands. Pride in her womanly capacity to please and echoes of her husband's delight will ultimately build pleasant emotional associations with sex for the woman, and usually will make passionate, orgasm-rewarded episodes frequent. The husband's freedom from pent-up pressures will make him much more capable of giving full satisfaction when passion finally develops.

Sexual technique with the unimpassioned woman must be somewhat forthright, since tickling caresses and teasing only excite an already-aroused partner. You need not prolong genital caresses, and should use gentle fluid-transferring caresses in preference to more violent ones. Use lubrication consistently for a few weeks and keep lubricants handy for several months. Actually, the amount of moisture in the vagina shows rather accurately a woman's state of passion, so that you can revise your approach in an effort to bring her to climax if your first genital caresses meet with slickly lubricated membranes. If you go ahead without impassioned response, remain in surface contact until lubrication and relaxation make entrance completely comfortable and keep to short strokes right at the female opening for some time. Such episodes usually prove quite satisfying to both partners when the wife acknowledges their loving-service nature instead of faking passion, although an occasional deception does no harm if you prefer.

Some women need repeated waves of sexual stimulation to arouse them. If there is any reason to believe that this might be your problem, you can either play off a few preliminary climaxes, concentrate sexual encounters into short, fast-paced periods or build up to climactic sex with several non-climactic episodes.

Sometimes concern about lack of response itself imposes crushing burdens upon a woman's ardor. Patient expectation during the early months of marriage or of sexual rehabilitation often wins ultimate orgasm-capped rewards. A slight scaling down of expectations often relieves a woman's concern about her nature.

Care to avoid sexual injury by either your husband's or your own fingernails often sets passion-quenching fears at rest, as does adequate and unfailing sexual lubrication. Painful intercourse with resulting sexual fears often results from readily corrected physical disease, which you should suspect if tenderness, excessive discharge, itching or a family pinworm problem accompany sexual difficulties. Emotional tangles and upsets can underlie lack of ardor, and may yield either to the measures outlined in Chapter Seven or to professional counseling. In some cases, specific methods of relaxation permit ardent response which tensions and conflicts would otherwise impede. Stepwise relaxation, tranquilizing tub baths, preliminary sleep and vacationing for sex often prove effective.

10.
How to Build
Potency and Increase
Male Capacities

Couple action can almost always ensure the man's capacity to carry through his sexual urges, and can usually increase the frequency with which such urges arise. Both partners play an active part in this program. The wife's role includes enhancing her own sex appeal, making sure that each episode builds pleasant associations with sex for her partner, and helping her husband toward sexual confidence. The husband's role includes modified sex techniques, efforts to decrease the amount of semen discharged in each sexual encounter, and steps to combat emotional blocks.

Spurring normal sex urges.

Episodes of impotence quite frequently stem entirely from defective provocation. The wife takes her husband for granted and makes no effort to keep herself attractive for him or to entice, excite and satisfy him sexually. The husband follows the same routine night after night, from the first kiss to the final grateful pat, without enough variety to bestir his woman's interest or to save himself from boredom. No wonder his penis, which remains erect only during periods of considerable sexual excitement, sometimes sags disappointingly!

No matter how much you want to get warm, you can't light a fire without the match. Psychologic desire is not the same as sexual excitement. A man who badly wants sexual relief may still find nothing to get excited about in the prospects before him. Thus when impotence plagues your sex life, you should definitely review your couple techniques for initiating and building sex excitement. Look through the early chapters of this book while you ask yourself questions like these:

¶ As a wife: "Am I doing everything I can to keep my appeal for my husband alive? Do I do my absolute best as a sex partner to excite him and please him? Exactly what could I do to give him a pleasant surprise the next time he makes advances?"

¶ As a husband: "Am I pushing myself toward sex when I don't have a genuine urge instead of waiting for the urge to develop? How can I vary the time, place and manner of my approach enough to keep us both from getting bored? Could I stir enough further response in my wife by more intensive techniques to make her a more exciting sex partner?"

You will probably find many practical methods with which you can provoke sufficiently intense sexual excitement to guarantee effective erection whenever a genuine urge exists. In applying these ideas, the chances are that you will build the number of urges quite substantially, too.

How to decrease discharge of semen.

If your potency problem stems from trying to keep up with your wife's desires, seminal retention may be the answer. You cannot build much sexual excitement until you have a charge of semen waiting for release. If you cut down the loss of semen in each episode, another charge accumulates quite quickly. This makes further sexual activity possible long before you would otherwise have power.

Neither husband nor wife suffers any great impairment of orgasm from seminal retention, which often substantially increases or even doubles the number of encounters possible. It does not affect fertility, and makes no difference in your program for birth control. The only real drawback is decreased and somewhat briefer sexual contentment: the man feels satisfied but not completely tranquil after retaining semen, and needs more sexual release quite soon and urgently at times.

When to retain semen.

Generally speaking, you should wait until you have mastered basic sexual technique and achieved a reasonably good couple adjustment before you try seminal retention. Even then, you should always let semen flow forth freely when you anticipate a separation or a period of sexual denial (as during the menstrual period if such is your custom) or if your wife's state of health limits her participation. However, you will probably find seminal retention useful on occasion, especially if your wife's desires exceed your own. Seminal retention often makes possible enough extra episodes to even out couple sex pace altogether under these circumstances.

Some husbands find that they can conserve semen with ease, and do so routinely. Most save this method for occasions when extra sexual activity seems likely to be desirable, as during periods of active feminine desire (which some women have at certain times of the menstrual month, especially just at the end of their flow), and during vacations, holiday seasons, or other times when experience has taught that mutual desire runs high. Relatively few find this method worthwhile merely to increase the number of episodes for purely selfish pleasure when their natural pace already more than fulfills their wive's desires.

The actual number of sexual encounters involved makes relatively little difference in deciding whether to release or retain semen, since couple desire varies widely. Don't use seminal retention to match your pace with a mythical "normal" level. Use it to suit your partnership needs.

How to get ready for seminal retention.

You should gain control of the necessary muscles before you attempt seminal retention during intercourse. The main muscles involved are those which surround the urinary tube at the bladder opening, whose normal action is to cut off the urinary stream. You can thus master control of these muscles by cutting off the urinary flow several times each time you empty your bladder. Other muscles involved lift the crotch area up into your body and surround the base of the penis. If you try to lift your testicles and the back of your scrotum straight up into your body, you will feel these muscles contract.

After you have learned to tighten these two sets of muscles at will (the cut-off muscle first, the lifting ones next), you can strengthen them by contracting them firmly for a few seconds several times daily. Since nobody can tell that you are doing this exercise, you can easily perform it while you are riding to work, finishing your morning coffee, or at any other convenient, easy-to-remember time.

How to practice seminal retention.

After you have learned to control the muscles involved, clamp off seminal discharge by tightening those muscles one night during your final surge. This action does not interfere with other sexual movements in any way, nor do such movements cut down the efficiency of the retention technique. Finish off the episode exactly as you would if you were letting go, but keep the muscles clamped around the bladder outlet from the beginning of your final surge until ejaculation is complete.

Building pleasant, conflict-free associations with sex.

Sexual excitement is basically an *emotional* rather than a purely *physical* phenomenon. The emotional element of any experience stems from the emotions you have previously felt in similar circumstances as well as from instinctive drives. A man who feels pleasurable security and pride in conjunction with sexual enterprise today will find sexual excitement potentiated with these emotions later. A man who feels guilt or anxiety in conjunction with sexual enterprise today will find sexual excitement somewhat tainted with these emotions thereafter. This effect is even greater in marriage than in many other areas because so many circumstances are common to each sexual event: the same partner, usually the same room, often the same time of night and so on.

As a couple, you can both build pleasant emotional associations with sex and avoid unpleasant or disturbing ones. You know what makes your partner feel secure and good: statements of love, compliments, harmonious discourse and so on (not to mention the affectionate display of sexual response itself). Certainly you can do your best to add these elements to the emotional flavor of sex contact. You also know what evokes unpleasant emotions like anxiety, anger, guilt and feelings of inadequacy in your partner. However, such feelings often arise in situations which involve some conflict of interest between husband and wife, so that you may find it harder to do what is best for the *couple* (and in the long run for both partners as individuals).

Perhaps the biggest problem centers on a wife's participation in sex when she has no sensual desire. Unless she makes her willingness entirely clear, her husband often finds these incidents tainting his attitudes toward sex with quite unpleasant feelings:

¶ Anxiety if he must always wonder whether each approach will meet rebuff.

¶ Indignation if rebuffs and hesitations seem to violate his rightful privileges (which in point of law and religion they always do, although the prevailing attitudes in our society might deny this position).

¶ Insecurity if he feels his wife's resentment as a threat to love and marriage.

¶ Guilt if he doubts the rightness of his act or feels that he has inflicted suffering and harm.

¶ Inadequacy if his idea of masculinity includes consistent capacity to inspire feminine response (which is a common erroneous attitude).

The resulting emotional tangles often impair potency even when the wife passionately desires intercourse, besides being disturbing in themselves. Both parties suffer as individuals, and the importance of sex as a welding tie in marriage decreases sharply.

Most women gladly give themselves in loving service whenever their husbands so desire once they realize the importance of this step to couple contentment. Such deference to the husband's pace is absolutely essential in cases of emotion-blocked male capacity, and generally worthwhile in any situation. However, a few wives have difficulty because of two fears which both partners can help to change.

Easiest to correct is *fear of intolerable demands*. When a wife holds her husband down to less intercourse than his sex pace demands, he generally makes some kind of tentative approach each night. She cannot help but think that he will continue to do so if she makes herself more readily available. At the same time, she foresees no increase in her own responsiveness and no change in the comfort and tolerability of her role in non-impassioned service, both of which are actually quite likely to occur. Therefore she sees herself ravished every night with no more sexual reward than she already gets, and cannot accept this prospect.

This picture is entirely false, but needs to be refuted by action instead of mere words. First of all, the husband must make sure that his wife's services always remain comfortable and convenient for her. He should lubricate well, make entrance gradually, and follow the other precautions detailed in the last chapter. Then the couple should try the free rein approach for two or three months in agreed experiment. The woman's main fear is that when she gives her man complete control she will never again get back to where she is if the alternative proves as bad as she expects. By making an agreement limited in time, she may overcome her hesitancy.

Fear for her human dignity, integrity and independence almost always plays some part in wifely restraint. Actually, the female role is in no way inconsistent with these things. When a man leads his partner through intricate dance steps, everyone knows her skill must match or exceed his to let her follow. Sex pace and participation must similarly be governed mainly by the male, but this dominance does not make her role in any way inferior. However, the popular notion of fifty-fifty in marriage means to most people that each and every burden, decision and responsibility is parceled out or equally shared, not that a couple should work as a team with each person playing a distinctly different role. This popular notion makes the wife's lead-following role seem like "second fiddle," and thus unsuited to her dignity and worth.

Once again, actions speak louder than words in fighting this concern. A husband must meet his wife's need for dignity and integrity day by day and hour by hour to make it psychologically possible for her to follow his lead in sex. He must prove to her that obedience to his desires in this respect will not lead to household enslavement. For instance, he might give her complete control of the household budget, not as a concession to repay her for letting him control the couple's sex pace but as recognition of her competence and authority in this sphere.

A woman who has trouble giving in to her husband can often meet her psychologic need for recognition with activities outside the realm of sex. She can run a household to be proud of, become a leader in church and school activities, get a job or build a career. She can take up a captivating and creative hobby or a sports interest in which one of her abilities makes her shine. She can prove her worth in many different ways, and her husband should compliment and acknowledge her achievements. The more she feels his recognition of her worth, the easier it is for her to do without much share in the command of their sex life.

Sexual confidence.

When a husband starts a sexual episode, he needs to feel sure of himself sexually. Any substantial doubt about either his capabilities at the moment or his worth as a sex partner dampens his ardor in a hurry. This is one reason why a constantly willing wife inspires increased potency—by her actions, she accepts him as a reliably good sex partner, which builds his confidence more than anything she (or I) could say. Both husband and wife can take further action in building sexual self-confidence, however. Several approaches usually prove worthwhile.

Knowledge of sex technique helps.

The parts of this book which you have already read should go a long way toward providing this aid. If you have not yet mastered basic sex technique, you may find that a certain amount of mental rehearsal helps you to be sure of yourself in bed. You shouldn't tie yourself to a set campaign, but you should go over the ground until you feel certain that you will never be at a loss for what to do at any stage of the proceedings.

Heartfelt compliments build confidence.

A heartfelt compliment always helps to quell self-doubt. A wife who has enjoyed full orgastic reward should obviously voice testimonials of her satisfaction and compliment her husband's virile force. No matter how intense her physical response, she should not take it for granted that he knows the way she feels: a few words and caresses reveal contentment and felicitate its source in ways which definitely benefit your husband's future powers.

Perhaps more important (and certainly more frequently neglected) are compliments for gentlemanly conduct of less directly satisfying bouts. A husband who has brought his wife to orgasm would score himself a sexual success even without her compliments. Not so the husband who has done well in less auspicious circumstances. Take the bridegroom who gives his partner a comfortable and easy introduction to sex, for instance: he deserves appreciation for his tender and well-managed attentions, even though his wife has known no joy and manifests no evidence of his success. Or take the impassioned husband who conducts himself in such a way that serving him becomes a comfortable communion instead of legalized rape. Can his wife not properly commend his skill and consideration?

Compliments mean the most in situations like these, when a husband can do the best possible job without inspiring the response which automatically proves his sexual worth. Without his wife's deliberate comment, the husband's achievement wins less than its deserved reward, and may even leave him suffering unjustly from a sense of failure or of guilt. One caution, though: compliments should be genuine, not spurious or exaggerated. Better to single out one single item of which the husband may be proud (for instance: "You certainly kept yourself under control for a long time tonight") than to praise him effusively for non-existent achievements (for instance: "You sure gave me a big thrill tonight" when he knows that he didn't). The intimacy of sexual communion allows much less deception than most people think, and even pretense in which both parties join is seldom truly successful.

Set reasonable standards of success.

Probably the biggest obstruction to sexual self-confidence today is the false notion that a competent husband brings his wife to orgasm every time he tries. I doubt if any man alive comes close to reaching this visionary goal. According to Dr. Kinsey, less than one-fifth of women reach an orgasm two times out of five, and most must be content with still less frequent orgastic reward. While you might improve upon these averages through the sex techniques detailed in this book, you should set your goal at freedom from unsatisfied sex yearnings and consider female orgasms as additional bonus treats, not minimum success.

What to do if couple measures fail to banish impotency.

A few husbands find that potency failures continue to plague them in spite of improved enticement and technique, seminal retention and home attack on emotional problems. If you find yourself in this group, you should arrange for an examination by your family doctor or by a specialist in urology. An infected prostate gland or some other medically correctable condition may be at fault. If no such explanation can be found, professional marriage or psychologic counseling may be your best bet. Episodes of impotence often stem from deep-lying psychologic problems. Perhaps the victim has profoundly disturbing emotional experiences linked in his mind with sex, or finds distaste from incidents in his early family life subconsciously attached to the marital relationship. Few people can unravel such tangles by themselves: the key problems remain locked deep in your brain's sub-basement vaults where only a skilled counselor can find his way. The types of counselors available are mentioned on page 133.

Chapter Ten's outline for action to improve
a husband's sexual capabilities.

When potency lags, you may have simply failed to provoke adequate excitement. The wife should enhance her physical appeal and both partners should seek new and exciting methods for allurement, caress and intercourse itself from the early chapters of this book.

A man whose natural sex pace does not match his wife's can often gain extra capacity through seminal retention. You should wait until you have mastered basic sex technique before applying this method. Learn the necessary muscular control and build up semen-retaining strength by interrupted urination and other exercises. Clamp down during the final sexual surge, and hold the muscles firm until ejaculation is complete.

Emotional associations can either help or hurt potency. You can both build pleasant emotional associations with sex in marriage and avoid unpleasant or disturbing ones. Episodes which the wife undertakes in loving service rather than in passionate desire most frequently cause problems. The husband can make it easier for his wife to accept him willingly (which she should try her best to do) by carefully preserving both her comfort and her pride during such encounters and otherwise. Both partners should build up the male's sexual confidence, the husband mainly by positive knowledge of sexual technique, the wife by freely voiced compliments and uninhibited response, and both together by setting reasonable standards for his performance.

If these measures fail, do not lose hope. A physician's examination may reveal a readily correctable disorder or a few sessions with a psychologic counselor may set you straight.

11.
How to
Conquer Periods of
Natural Constraint

No matter how hard you try, you cannot perpetually hold yourselves ready to fulfill each other's sexual needs. Separations, illnesses, pregnancies, and other natural constraints often keep either husband or wife from unrestrained service to the other's sexual desires. Several special techniques help you to survive these periods or overcome the difficulties they impose without undue upheaval.

Intercourse during menstruation.

Many couples regard menstruation as an absolute barrier to sexual communion. Ordinarily, this restriction does no great harm. However, couples who must fit their sex life into schedules over which they have no control (such as brief periods available between business trips) or couples who rely on rhythm for birth control often find themselves stuck with such a short open season that sexual indulgence on the last two or three days of menstruation becomes almost necessary. Suppose, for example, that a woman has six days of menstrual flow and a twenty-six-day cycle.

If she avoids intercourse during menstruation, then skips the seventh to the seventeenth days to reduce fertility, she imposes a pattern of eight days open season followed by seventeen days closed. Unless her husband has a very slow pace indeed, he will be climbing the walls from unrequited desire during the fertile period and hair-trigger fast from pent-up congestion when his wife finally becomes available. Indulgence during the menstrual flow often seems better than continual sexual disharmony in such circumstances.

Sometimes fairly rapid-paced couples or couples who find that mutual ardor commonly arises at that time of the month also disregard the popular taboo against sex during menstruation. Actually, no harm whatever results from having relations at this time provided that:

¶ Neither party has strong and unchangeable emotional aversion to this practice:

¶ You avoid indulgence during delayed or abnormal bleeding which might possibly indicate a threatened miscarriage or some other condition in which intercourse might prove harmful.

¶ The husband carefully avoids direct or indirect transfer of mouth moisture to his wife's genitals (for instance, by using saliva as a lubricant or by alternating mouth-to-breast, hand-to-breast and hand-to-genital play).

If you proceed with sexual indulgence during menstruation, you will find that the increase in blood supply to the female organs during intercourse considerably increases menstrual blood loss for a few minutes. For this reason, you should probably abstain for the first day or two, as long as flow is fairly heavy anyway. A rubber sheet or plastic mattress cover helps to preserve your mattress. You can buy disposable plastic-backed pads at any large drug store or hospital supply house in various sizes and thicknesses. One of these beneath your hips avoids a great deal of mess. Provision for donning a sanitary pad after intercourse makes sense. This brief interruption in afterplay seldom proves disturbing to either partner. Wives whose religious beliefs permit mechanical or chemical birth control measures find use of the diaphragm somewhat unpleasant during menstruation, so most couples switch to suppositories, jellies or rubbers for birth control. The douche recommended on the morning after suppository or jelly use can be replaced, if you wish, with a pitcher douche, in which you pour lukewarm water across the genital opening rather than insert a douche tip.

Pregnancy.

Early pregnancy has an almost unpredictable effect on wifely ardor. Some women feel a sense of pleasant release from pregnancy fears which aids their ardor. Other women find their passionate interest distinctly curbed. This should cause no undue concern: sexual desire and responsiveness will return fairly soon.

Abdominal protuberance does not usually interfere in any way with sexual activity until about the fifth month. At this point, pressure on the abdomen may create discomfort or impede breathing. Placing one or two pillows under the woman's hips during husband-on-top episodes usually helps. Positions in which she draws up her knees somewhat or locks her ankles behind her husband's back may prove comfortable for a time. You may find the face to face lying-on-your-sides position quite useful, too.

By the seventh and eighth months, most women find that they cannot make sexual motions very well in any position. The husband-on-top position still works well so long as the woman can remain comfortable with her knees drawn far up, but in the latter part of pregnancy this position almost cuts off breathing. At this point, most couples must go over to either the crossed position or the husband-from-the-rear posture. The wife should keep her hands very active during sex play and during intercourse to add what she can to her husband's satisfaction. Her husband should caress the clitoris almost constantly during intercourse whenever she shows any evidence of being aroused, since sexual frictions themselves seldom give her full satisfaction in the available positions.

Your family doctor or obstetrician will probably advise you to avoid sexual intercourse for the last few weeks before the baby comes. He wants the upper birth passage to remain germ-free, and intercourse transports ever-present germs from the female opening up into the passage. Since you can't resolve sexual excitement in the usual way, you should probably try to keep from arousing too much sexual interest. If ardor develops on either side of the fence, there is no medical objection to intimate or even climax-generating sex play so long as caresses or genital frictions involve no penetration into the vagina.

Tenderness after pregnancy.

If no tears or deliberate cuts require stitches after childbirth, cautious sexual contact usually proves comfortable after three weeks. Sexual activity need not be restrained in any way after six weeks.

Stitches require a somewhat more cautious approach. The doctor who delivers your first baby (and often later ones, too) almost always has to make a scissors cut at the female opening to provide enough room for easy delivery. This cut prevents irreparable stretching of tissue and makes hard-to-repair tears much less likely. It also allows him to snug up the opening after delivery is complete by taking tucks in the exposed muscle layers. A deliberate opening-enlarging cut definitely helps to preserve the wife's husband-pleasing capacities in most cases, but it does leave the wife with a tender spot for several weeks.

After delivery, the wife should frequently test her state of tenderness, and keep her husband informed about it. A great many couples get into a heat of passion before discovering that the female organ still remains quite tender, and then face the prospect of either leaving each other in a state of over-excitement or resuming their sex life on an unfortunate note. Don't be afraid to try various forms of finger stretching and friction on your own organ after the first two or three weeks: you won't do yourself any harm, and may well discover residual soreness which makes further postponement of sexual contact wise.

After three weeks without stitches or four to six weeks with any considerable tear or cut, you should find that almost any form of self-manipulation causes no sharp discomfort. You may find that one area along the back of the vaginal opening (which is the location in which most doctors place deliberate opening-enlarging cuts) remains very tender to even surface touch. This usually signifies that a tiny nerve fibril was caught in one of the stitches or damaged during delivery. Such bruised nerve tenderness disappears very slowly, usually over a period of six months to a year, so you cannot wait until it is gone before resuming relations. If you have a problem of this kind, get a tube of Surfacaine ointment for use in place of lubricant. Apply it to the affected area before each possible intercourse, and again during advanced sex play if finger frictions cause discomfort.

Barring a bruised nerve problem, the vagina should cease to give discomfort from surface frictions within three weeks. Stretching or pressure on the muscles around the opening, especially at the site of a tear or deliberate cut, may cause discomfort for another week or so. Hot sitz baths often help speed healing at this point. Sit in four inches of hot water for thirty minutes every evening, adding a little extra hot water at intervals to keep the temperature high. Always test with your hand or some other unimmersed part when adding hot water, since immersed areas become so inured to heat that you might otherwise burn yourself. Wrap a dry towel around your shoulders if necessary to keep warm: the hot water often makes you sweat all over, and the exposed parts of your body may become chilly.

Hot sitz baths not only speed healing of bruised muscles but also relax and soothe them temporarily. Take a hot sitz bath just before your first excursion into sex after childbirth even if you have noted no muscular tenderness. This first episode also may go better with Surfacaine ointment as lubricant, copious extra lubrication, and all the other precautions advised to prevent discomfort among newlyweds (Chapter Four). One slight variation: be sure to lubricate the shaft of the penis instead of just its head, since most discomfort involved in sexual intercourse after delivery comes from pressures and frictions of the penis against the back rim of the female opening rather than from initial entrance.

If your doctor has made a deliberate opening-enlarging cut, you will find that positions thrusting the shaft of the penis back against the rear rim of the vagina continue to cause discomfort for several weeks or months. The wife's-heels-on-husband's-shoulders and the wife's-knees-drawn-up variations usually prove unusable. If wifely discomfort occurs during intercourse in any other position, a slight shift to bring the angle of male entry around a bit farther toward the front usually solves the problem. In the standard husband-on-top posture, this means that the wife can let her legs down a litle straighter or that the husband can move his hips to make his angle of approach from above his wife's hip area instead of from down between her thighs.

Like the honeymoon, the period of readjustment after childbirth involves a period of sacrificial self-control on the part of the husband. For several weeks, he must settle for the modest sexual relief which he can get without causing his wife discomfort if he wants to rebuild couple satisfaction soon. This sacrifice pays off manyfold in speeding and increasing the level of ardent response his wife can give thereafter. However, the wife should appreciate her husband's kindness in putting her comfort ahead of his pent-up desires and try to diminish his sacrifice. She should conscientiously exercise both her abdominal muscles (as her doctor will direct) and the muscles of her genital organs (with the procedures given in Chapter Five) to restore her husband-pleasing potential. She should make herself attractive to her husband with grooming aids, bedtime allurement and attire instead of letting sex appeal take a complete back seat to motherhood. She should deliberately excite his sexual urges and supplement his sexual gratifications with the caresses and maneuvers described in the first few chapters of this book. If he treats her gently, the least she can do is keep his gentleness from completely depriving him of satisfaction.

Illness.

A severe illness often calls for a decrease in vigorous sexual activity or for a shift to lower-key, less strongly exciting means of getting sexual relief. The crossed or husband-from-the-rear-while-lying-on-your-sides postures seem reasonably apt. Although it sounds backwards, the wife can often help keep down the vigor of her husband's efforts by taking a bit more initiative: if she gets him to the point of erection so that he can get relief without taking a very active role in preliminary sex play, his energy expenditure usually remains low. The wife-astride postures involve more vigorous movement by the male than most couples realize, however, so that the wife's initiative should usually cease when time comes for sexual entrance.

If a disorder of the sex organs themselves (for instance, a minor operation on the mouth of the uterus) prevents sexual contact for a long period, the non-penetrating use of surface friction may give relief. The husband can approach from either the front or the rear, lay his well-lubricated penis against his wife's genitals, and let her thighs fall together across its lower surface to encompass his organ, gaining a degree of sexual release. Some couples play each other past a climax (in this case using the otherwise forbidden up-

and-down caresses of the penile shaft combined with snakebites, frenulum pinches and other methods whose use must usually be restrained to prevent a too-fast climax), which is both proper and helpful in this instance. Remember that any sexual service between husband and wife is perfectly normal so long as it does not replace intercourse as the ideal objective.

Some sexual difficulties during prolonged illness may be due to medicines rather than to illness itself. Potency or desire for sex rarely or never are sharply involved, but the amphetamines (which are commonly used as stimulants, for asthma or for weight reduction) may lead to prolonged erection and considerable extra need for stimulation to produce a climax. Drugs given for nervousness, sleeplessness, epilepsy and high blood pressure also may have sex-disturbing effects. Although many patients worry about the effect of medicines on their sex life when no such action exists, you should always check such suspicions with your doctor. If medicines have anything to do with your trouble, he can usually substitute something which works just as effectively on your disease but does not have adverse sexual effects.

Separations.

Before marriage age, almost all men and most women relieve excessive sexual tensions through self-manipulation. One survey showed that ninety-two per cent of men and sixty to seventy per cent of women admit to self-relief through some form of masturbation (see Stone and Stone, A MARRIAGE MANUAL, p. 221). These figures are probably low, since people usually shade their replies toward the answer they consider proper in such surveys and since many forms of self-relief common among young women involve actions which they might not think of as masturbation, such as assumption of strained postures in which muscle quiverings lead to sexual release.

Modern medical science strongly supports the view that masturbation does no harm to the sex organs (so long as any implements used in female self-relief are smooth and unbreakable). Psychologic harm results only if the individual's attitudes and beliefs make masturbation a source of guilt or anxiety.

If you have profound convictions or beliefs opposing masturbation, best avoid it. If you have doubts, discuss them with your religious adviser. Otherwise, masturbation may occasionally have a valid place in your marriage, as it probably had in your youth. No matter how willingly you both try to meet the other's sexual needs, circumstances and health problems may keep you from achieving this goal at times. Prolonged physical separations or the necessity for denial during pregnancy, illness and so on certainly lead to less social misbehavior if sexual tensions remain at a safe level. Masturbation affords one medically safe and harmless means of achieving that goal, if your particular religious beliefs or moral principles do not deny it to you.

The menopause.

A woman does not lose her capacity to enjoy sex with the menopause. Although she feels no further urgent desire for sexual gratification, she gets just as much satisfaction as ever from intercourse. In fact, many women find the menopause a release from previous pregnancy fears and concerns. They can relax so much more thoroughly after birth control worries and maneuvers cease that both their effectiveness as sex partners and their pleasure in the act greatly improve.

Nevertheless, the menopause sometimes brings sex problems. While it probably does not cause sex-disturbing moodiness and other emotional upsets by physical or glandular changes, the menopausal period is a time of great stress and strain. The menopause ends hope for further family, and brings women face to face with the advancing family-life void. The need for a new approach to life often proves upsetting, even though hormonal changes themselves do not cause great distress. Nervousness and blue moods often upset the delicate emotional balance required for ideal sexual indulgence.

If emotional disturbances around the menopause do not require psychiatric care, you can usually control their sex-disrupting action with continuous tubs (see Chapter Nine) or with mood-lifting or tranquilizing medications which your family doctor can prescribe. A woman in her forties should train herself to plan, work for, and anticipate pleasant experiences in the future instead of dwelling on failures of the past. Her husband should provide compassionate companionship, but should not try to buck her up with foolish injunctions. Loss of capacity to procreate is just as real to a family-centered woman as loss of his right arm would be to a baseball star. She has a right to mourn for a little while, and to receive sympathy instead of prodding while she readjusts her views on life.

The male menopause involves a sharper break in couple sex life. Ten to fifteen years after his wife's reproductive retirement, the male gradually ceases to have either sex interest or capacity. Most couples gracefully accept this change when it occurs, since hormones, prostatic massage and all of the other measures sometimes recommended have little or no actual effect.

Summary of advice on periods of natural constraint.

When an adverse situation or your birth control method limits sexual activity too stringently, don't hesitate to commune during the last two days of the menstrual period.

During advanced pregnancy, use positions which shift the husband's angle of entry slightly or which shift both partners over onto their sides. Build excitement with various caresses to make up for impaired sex appeal and clumsiness in sexual movement. Most couples do best by avoiding sexual stimulation after medical orders prohibit intercourse, but intensely intimate caresses sometimes give a degree of release if you inadvertently become aroused.

Tenderness after delivery lasts much longer if stitches were used. The wife should test for tenderness before encouraging her husband's advances. If surface soreness persists more than two or three weeks in one spot, try Surfacaine ointment. Hot sitz baths often speed healing after the first three weeks, too.

Lubricate the shaft of the penis as well as the head in early sexual episodes after childbirth. Avoid positions which thrust the shaft of the penis against the back rim of the female opening. Lay groundwork for future sexual delights through a gentle masculine approach and through deliberate feminine allurement and caress in the early weeks after childbirth.

When prolonged illness restrains your couple sex

life, the crossed and husband-from-the-rear-while-lying-on-your-sides postures are most apt. When disorders of the genitals prevent normal sexual contact, release through otherwise-prohibited forms of climax-generating sex play seems perfectly proper. If medicines seem in any way at fault, check with your doctor.

In periods of prolonged separation or inescapable sexual denial, there is no medical objection to self-relief through masturbation. If you have doubts about the moral and religious aspects of self-relief, discuss them with your religious adviser.

After the menopause, a woman usually has no pressing sexual urge or desire, but she can respond just as thoroughly as ever (and sometimes more so) to masculine advances. Emotional problems during the menopausal period respond to special baths, medicines and other measures. Compassion helps more than injunctions to buck up.

12.
Perfect Pacing

Complete couple harmony involves three different types of pacing:

¶ Means of synchronizing sex movements during intercourse.

¶ Measures to slow or speed each other's build-up to climax so that you both arrive simultaneously.

¶ Techniques for bringing divergent levels of desire into line.

The previous chapters of this book touch upon most of the specific methods you can use for these purposes. In this chapter, you will find these ideas pulled together and summarized for ready reference.

How to synchronize sex movements.

Since the husband usually provides the basic in and out rhythm upon which all sex movement is built, the wife has to synchronize her motions with his.

The standard husband-on-top posture usually proves a good starting point for learning this skill. After sexual entrance, the husband can poise himself with the penis barely inserted so that his wife's early efforts will not bring him to a rapid conclusion. She places one or both hands on his hips to improve her consciousness of his position. By rocking her hips forward as if she were trying to look at her female organ without raising her back off the bed, she both alters the angle of her husband's entrance and slides an inch or so up the penis shaft. With a little practice, she can make this motion entirely with the muscles of her buttocks and lower abdomen. Contraction of the upper abdominal muscles impedes breathing, and contraction of the back muscles (which seems almost instinctive, so that it must be consciously fought) both makes her stiff as a partner and quickly tires her out.

When the wife can rock easily without undue fatigue, the husband should start slow and moderate in and out movement, generally with one stroke either in or out to correspond to every two or three complete cycles of female movement. He can often guide her rhythm with clucking noises or clutching caresses. After both parties get the sense of rhythm, the husband can change the speed or extent of his movement, with the wife following his lead. Probably you will need several episodes to make this movement seem so natural that you can carry through to a climax without letting instinct take over.

Most couples enjoy ordinary rock and thrust movement sufficiently to stick with it for several months, during which they master various positions, harmonies, and rhythms together. After reaching this point, you might go back to the fundamental position

again and learn to roll instead of rock. See page 93
for details of this technique.

How to get into tandem before a sex climax.

Better timing of your build-up toward a sex climax
depends mainly on caresses and sex movements which
spur one partner along more rapidly than the other.
You can delay an impending climax for a few seconds
by stopping all sexual motion and friction, but such
tactics generally prove too little and too late. If you
want to finish together, you should try to stay together
all the way from the beginning, adjusting your techniques either to speed your own relative progress
toward climax or to speed your partner's progress
without over-accelerating your own.

When the husband seems ahead of his wife.

Caresses with the fingertips, stimulating the nipple
between rolled-in lips and rolling the knuckle of your
thumb against the clitoris generally speed your wife's
progress toward a climax without affecting your own.

Another useful technique is surface friction between the genitals. The husband approaches from
straight above his wife's hips with his penis more or
less at right angles to the female opening instead of in
alignment with it. Ordinary sex motions will then
slide the top surface of the penis along the clitoris and
inner lips, which are very sensitive sexually. The
frenulum and other keen trigger areas of the penis do
not rub against anything unless the wife puts her legs
down straight and squeezes her thighs together, which
she should not do in this particular maneuver.

You can shift to ordinary intercourse gradually from surface friction. The husband drops his hips between his wife's legs for a short penetrating stroke or two and then returns to further surface friction. He alternates the varieties of friction until he feels certain that she has caught up.

Buttock massage during intercourse also speeds the woman toward climax without particularly affecting the man. While easiest to carry out in a wife-astride position, buttock massage also works well in lying-on-sides positions or (by rolling the wife slightly on her far side) in the crossed posture. Gentle, rhythmic stroking from the outside in, from the inside out or from the upper inner corner diagonally down to the side of the thigh prove most effective at first. Deeper stroking and kneading boost excitement late in intercourse. Firm clutching caresses work best to boost the climax itself rather than spur progress toward it.

After achieving full penetration, the husband can stir his wife's progress without pushing himself too far by pressing the top of the penile shaft firmly against the clitoris and writhing from side to side. This action catches the clitoris between the impinging penis and the pelvic bone underneath, giving deep pressure as well as surface friction. The penile area involved is the least sensitive one sexually, preventing overstimulation of the male.

Twitching of the deeply inserted penis often helps a woman over the final hump without pushing the male into climax, especially in the misaligned postures. In the wife's-heels-on-husband's-shoulders posture, for instance, the head of the penis presses sharply against the front vaginal wall, which is quite sexually sensitive in experienced women. The base of the penis presses back against the rear rim of the vagina, which also gives keen sexual sensation. A penile twitch thrills the woman in this position almost as much as an in-and-out movement, but hardly stimulates the man at all.

The wife herself can take several steps when she thinks her husband is getting ahead of her. During late sex play, a woman actually must continue caresses or her husband cannot possibly maintain excitement without intercourse. Too many women stop all forms of intimate caress for fear of carrying their husbands too far, and thus actually force their husbands to make sexual entry without taking extra time for wife-stimulating play. Caress with palms, tongue and moist, out-turned lips. Caress parts which you find exciting, including your husband's chest, his firm hip and thigh muscles, the top surface of his erect penis, or anything you have learned to link with masculine prowess. Above all, don't fade back into passivity in hopes of spurring further stimulation. Retreat if you want, but make it active, playful retreat, not seeming apathy.

Playful retreat remains your best maneuver if your husband shifts into position before you feel prepared. There's no rejection in a phrase like "Not quite yet" if it's combined with clawed finger caresses of his lower belly and followed by a chain of kisses or bites down his bared chest. Such actions are much more exciting than doubtful acquiescence, and still bring you extra minutes of husbandly caress.

After your husband makes his sex entry, one of the best ways to slow him up is actually to encourage him in further "upstairs" caress. Very few men will refuse an impassioned interval of mouth-to-mouth play or an around-the-world flurry of wifely caress. An embrace which presents your breast for kisses keenly excites and delights him even as it temporarily halts his sex-movements, especially if it is combined with tickling of his exposed sex organs or other intimate caress. You can trade *play* for *further male attentions* at any time without pushing your husband toward a climax, which usually comes mainly from sex frictions and almost entirely from genital rather than other bodily trigger areas.

In certain positions, especially the astride and sitting ones, a wife can writhe from side to side with her clitoris pressed back against the penile shaft. This motion seldom spurs a man to climax, but gives keen feminine delight.

Finally, a woman often can encourage extra caresses and stimulations by placing her man's hand in place upon her sexually sensitive parts. Most men find this a very exciting gesture, equivalent to intimate caress and not in any sense unwelcome. Lay his hand on your breast or buttock, cup your own breast in your hand and rub its nipple against his chest, rub his palm up along the inside of your thigh. In every sex position, you will find it possible to encourage welcome caresses when you feel extra desire for them.

When the wife seems ahead of her husband.

Occasionally, a short-fused woman wants to reach fruition without risky delays. But she does not want to challenge her husband's masterful control of the sexual situation by telling him to make entry before he feels so inclined. Two forms of genital caress are almost guaranteed to solve this problem: the snake bite type of wringing caress at the junction of the penile head and shaft, and the painfully pinching caress of the frenulum. Don't use these measures until you are ready for action, though. They don't fit in with later playful retreat.

A wife who gets far ahead of her husband creates no real problem. He can easily push her to climax with a few penile twitches or some short, sharp strokes, lie with her quietly for a minute or two, and then resume action. With reasonable care, he can hold off his climax until she is ready to repeat.

If your wife seems a little bit ahead, you can catch up quite easily with a few full-length, in-and-out strokes. Unless you both want a quick climax, though, why hurry? Her climax will almost always bring you along if you're that close, and once you push yourself over the brink there's no way on earth to slow back down again.

A woman seldom wants to rush her man when she is in a passion, and really shouldn't push him when she is not. If you can help your husband to achieve complete control when you come to him out of loving service, he will multiply your own delights in later episodes. If you find yourself growing tired, simply ask for an interval of rest and shift to a less active position for a few minutes.

Meeting each other's sexual desires.

Most couples draw constantly closer to one another in their level of sexual desire once they have mastered the basic techniques set forth in this book. A woman who indulges solely to please her husband in most early encounters usually develops passionate response ultimately, and craves sexual contact almost as often as her husband wants to give it. A man who tries to meet his wife's desire for frequent orgasm by prolonging contact and undertaking non-climactic episodes or by retaining semen to increase his capabilities soon finds himself so accustomed to these procedures that he would consider his sex life almost barren without them. Serious disparities of sex pace usually vanish after a few months of skillful couple endeavor, so long as each of you does his or her best to adapt to and please his partner. The problems definitely diminish through the years, if you keep them from causing excessive distress through these maneuvers:

If a man wants sex more often than the woman.

The *man* can help by always letting go rather than retaining semen, by making his advances entirely comfortable and reasonably convenient even when they are not passionately desired, by maintaining his physical attractiveness with good grooming and setting as good a domestic framework as possible for lively sex life. Detailed techniques can be found in Chapter Two through Six.

The *woman* can help by doing her best to attract and please her husband even when her own state of passion prevents orgastic reward. The resulting improved couple relationship and the gradual conversion of pride in feminine capability into passionate involvement and desire will almost always solve her problem.

If the woman wants sex more often than the man.

The *man* can increase her yield of orgasms by playing off one or two during preliminaries; by conducting the couple's sex life in waves of mounting excitement and release, starting with intimate play episodes, moving on to non-climactic ones (at least non-climactic for him, but involving orgasm for his wife whenever possible), and ending with a climactic episode for both; by seminal retention to increase his sexual capacities; and perhaps by changes in birth control method, sex position and technique to stimulate her more keenly during each sex episode.

The *woman* can help by accentuating her allure and desirability; by insisting upon and introducing variety and excitement into the couple's sex play and activity; and by taking the astride or chairbound posture fairly often, either writhing with her clitoris pressed down upon the top of the penile shaft or keeping largely to surface frictions for one or two waves of gratification before going on to mutual climax.

The gist of Chapter Twelve's advice on pacing.

In order to synchronize her sexual movements with her mate's, a wife usually needs to learn pacing skills with her husband poised above her in standard but superficial sexual contact, preferably on occasions when passion does not drive her toward hasty or instinctive acts. Learn the rock-and-thrust movements first, guided in rhythm by a hand on your husband's hip and perhaps by his clucking sounds or pace-matching caresses. Use these motions for a few months before trying to roll the pelvis in vertical circles during sexual contact.

In order to reach a climax together, you have to speed your own or your partner's lagging progress during sex play or early contact. Last minute measures inevitably fail. If the husband seems ahead at an early stage, he can caress his wife's neck with his fingertips, her breast with rolled-in lips, or her clitoris with his thumb knuckle. Surface friction between genitals often excites his wife without speeding his own climax. Buttock massage during intercourse also helps. Side-to-side writhing boosts women along toward orgasm, as does twitching of the deeply inserted penis.

The wife who feels herself lagging must continue active caresses during late sex play in order to maintain her husband's erection and let him give her the stimulation she needs. Playful retreat helps, but it must be *playful* and it must be physically *active*. Wanton feminine caresses often distract him even after sexual entry, and bring on further intervals of play. Side-to-side writhing with the clitoris pressed back on the penile shaft gives extra feminine pleasure during intercourse in some positions. Placing your husband's hand on areas you want caressed often proves quite effective either before or during intercourse.

If the wife seems ahead of her husband before sexual entry, she can bring him along fast with penile snake-bites or frenulum pinches. When she is far out in front, he can usually push her into a climax without ending the episode, then build up for a keenly mutual climax later.

Probably the best thing a wife can do if she finds herself exhausted is to ask her partner to shift to a more restful posture briefly rather than hurry him toward a climax.

In order to bring your sexual desires into tandem, you can use allurement, seminal retention, nonclimactic episodes and special techniques of sex play and participation as outlined in earlier chapters. Passion develops through willing sexual contact, so that a willing woman usually develops a pace very close to her husband's over a period of time. Male techniques for giving extra feminine orgasms also become second nature quite soon.

13.

Step by Step Method for Successfully Commencing, Redeeming or Improving Sexual Communion

When you set out to establish, rehabilitate or improve the physical side of your marriage, you can't put everything you have learned from this book into action at once. You need a step by step program. Take these seven steps toward total, consistent sexual success, being sure that each is thoroughly complete before you move on to the next. Remember that complete development of couple skills and adaptations takes literally years. Work patiently toward that goal in stages, and you will almost certainly achieve success.

STEP ONE: *Prepare.*

Before a sexual situation ever arises, you can take several steps to aid its chance for success.

A woman with little or no sexual experience usually should arrange stretching or removal of the virginal membrane (pages 64-7).

Both partners should master the technique of part-by-part relaxation (page 87). Wives find this technique very useful when sexual fears, household worries or emotional upheavals make them tense before a sexual episode, when pregnancy fears or momentary discomforts make them tighten up during a marital encounter, and occasionally when the husband's rapid progress toward a climax makes necessary a pause in sexual activity. Husbands use part-by-part relaxation mainly to halt too-rapid progress toward orgasm.

The birth control issue deserves thorough discussion well in advance of marriage, and thorough review if sexual relations have proved unsatisfactory. Couples with religious scruples about mechanical aid and chemical contraceptives usually use the rhythm method explained in Chapter Seven, possibly zeroed in through basal temperature determination for a couple of months. If rhythm involves an excessively long period of sexual drought (as it often does in women with an average cycle under twenty-six days) you may have to indulge in sex during the final two days of the menstrual period, using the suggestions on pages 182-4. Couples without religious scruples against mechanical and chemical methods generally prefer the diaphragm-jelly method at first. The bride should arrange for careful fitting of the diaphragm and for instruction from her family doctor or gynecologist several weeks beforehand if possible. After six months to one year, changed patterns of sexual sensitivity often make the diaphragm an impediment, especially to the woman. You might occasionally try a method using suppositories or jelly alone (Chapter Seven) preferably during the last few days before menstruation (to add rhythm method safety during your first experiments with an unfamiliar technique). Most couples find the difference quite marked after a few months of reasonably satisfying sexual cohabitation, and change control techniques accordingly.

Revamping faulty attitudes toward sex is one of

the most important preliminaries to mutually satisfying couple adjustment. Almost all women feel concerned about the possibility that a pregnancy will
result from a sexual episode. Even if they want children, the established plan and pattern of their lives
will change abruptly and profoundly with a pregnancy. This fact rather than fear of pregnancy itself
often underlies sex-impeding concern. Frank discussion of what life will be like if a pregnancy should
occur often gives relief (pages 113-15).

Emotional constraints upon sex life often stem from
faulty ideas planted in childhood to reinforce the
prevailing moral code. Little girls learn that it is
wrong to respond to men's advances, that they should
hide their nudity, that they should never handle their
sex organs or let others do so, and a dozen other rules
to which marriage makes exception. Little boys learn
that good girls are not sexually available and vice
versa without realizing that the best wives and mothers
can be perfect bed-fellows within the framework of
marriage. The attitudes that there is something wrong,
harmful, immodest or sinful about sex seldom are
taught in a form which specifies extra-marital sex.
You often have to review your present attitudes, the
sources of those attitudes and past experiences which
reveal those attitudes quite thoroughly (pages 128-33)
before freeing yourself from their constraint.

Finally, make sure that the circumstances for sexual
communion presage well for its success. Mood, en-
vironment and preliminary allurement contribute a
great deal to sexual excitement. Absolute privacy and
comfortable facilities also help. Be sure that you have
lubricants available—Surfacaine ointment during early
encounters or when recent childbirth has left slight

rawness, K-Y Jelly if your birth control technique involves a diaphragm or rubber, and unmedicated petroleum jelly otherwise.

STEP TWO: *Achieve comfortable and controlled communion.*

A woman must usually give herself in loving service to her husband for weeks or months before sexual awakening brings orgastic rewards, and occasionally thereafter. Her willingness to fulfill the feminine role without the spurs of passion or the promise of ecstatic joy ultimately opens the floodgates of sexual delight for herself as well as for her husband. However, she cannot easily sustain this willingness in the face of pain, or when experience has frequently taught her to expect pain.

Every couple should start their sex life, or start toward its rehabilitation if past efforts have proved unsatisfactory, with a solemn pact. The wife should agree to do her best to accommodate and please her husband whether she feels passionately inspired or not. The husband should agree to make every episode as completely comfortable for her as is humanly possible. This usually means use of artificial lubrication, relatively restful postures and cautious introduction of the male sex organ into the vagina for several weeks or months during the honeymoon or during the rehabilitation phase. Even if vaginal caresses show copious natural juices and a thoroughly relaxed vagina in an intensely aroused woman, last-moment reflexes can clamp down the vagina to make male entry painful. It is better to err on the side of excess lubrication and caution for a few weeks or months and accept a lower level of gratification in some episodes than to establish or revive satisfaction-wrecking feminine fears.

Cautious and gentle sexual indulgence also allows the husband to learn sexual control. A man who can maintain sex contact and activity until he decides to end the episode instead of letting biological pressures carry him quickly to an ungoverned conclusion multiplies both his own gratification and his wife's chance for orgastic delight. You'll find full details in Chapter Five.

Get in the habit of keeping each other informed and obeying each other's signals to aid couple control. Mastery over biological pressures is usually the only way to continue sexual contact until both partners get full satisfaction. Control thus rates at the top of your list after feminine comfort. Even if lags in motion or lessened depth of contact threaten the wife with loss of passion, she should go along with her husband's signals and desires. The worst that can happen to her in this way is subsidence of feeling without orgastic satisfaction, and there is a considerable chance that she will still be able to get what she wants. Body motions when her husband desires a freeze usually produce a lightning conclusion for him and total left-in-the-clouds frustration for her.

Don't get worried at this stage if sexual gratifications fail to fulfill your expectations. A wife gets only the satisfaction of bringing pleasure and contentment to someone she loves in most episodes at this stage. The husband gets somewhat more pleasure, but nothing approaching the gratification of intense and harmonious marital communion. You lay the groundwork for a sound sexual future by concentrating first on comfort and control. Bide your time hopefully. Keener pleasures will soon come.

STEP THREE: *Build more intensive climaxes.*

When consistently painless sexual service has thoroughly soothed the wife's sexual fears and when frequently proved control has given the husband confidence, you can shift your goal from fundamentals to an intense build-up of mutual sexual excitement. Some couples find themselves ready for this step in a week or two, others not for several months. Reread Chapters One through Six whenever you feel ready to take this next step.

At this stage, all couples, whether newly-married or experienced, can follow certain principles. Caresses before and during intercourse should be continual and intense. Each partner should take either an active or a passive role in sex movement at any one time instead of attempting synchronized couple motions. The person on top usually plays the active role in most positions, with the man usually taking the reins in on-your-sides postures. Your big problem will probably be the lag in feminine excitement during control-necessitated pauses, which you can handle with the techniques spelled out on pages 88-91. Precise timing will fail quite commonly at first: feel free to use intercourse-simulating sex play after the male climax in order to gain feminine satisfaction. Never leave the wife hanging if she remains highly excited. When she barely misses orgasm, congestion will not subside until strong sex play carries her over the brink.

Choice of postures in this stage depends somewhat on past sex experience and success. Newlyweds usually find positions which bring the penis into contact with the clitoris more effective than those which feature angulated alignment, pressure of the penile tip forward against the urinary tube and so on. The standard husband-on-top, face to face lying-on-sides and modified astride postures (pp. 67-75) usually prove apt. If the vagina has stretched well enough to make the standard astride and chair-borne postures comfortable, they offer advantages at times. Couples who have had considerable sexual experience often find the wife's-heels-on-husband's-shoulders and the wife's-knees-drawn-up postures especially appropriate at this stage (pp. 80-2). These postures allow keen stimulation of the fully-awakened woman, and their sole disadvantage, lack of feminine movement, makes no difference while you are letting one party supply all the activity anyway.

By exploring various combinations of movement and caress without introducing the complexities of synchronized couple movement, most couples can achieve mutual satisfaction fairly consistently within a few weeks or months. Some women do not experience orgasm no matter how high their excitement mounts, requiring a gradual tapering afterplay on all occasions. Most women reach orgasm frequently (but not always) on occasions which they undertake in the heat of passion rather than in loving service. However, almost every couple gets together occasionally when mutual orgasm is clearly unattainable from the start, and an occasional loss of feminine passion during pauses necessitated by male control seems inevitable. Do not regard a few such incidents as failures or inadequacies.

STEP FOUR: *Attack sexual difficulties.*

Use the trouble-shooting chapters in this book (Chapters Seven through Ten) to settle any basic difficulties before proceeding further. You may be conscious of faulty attitudes and emotional upheaval in association with sex, or may suspect the presence of such factors only through failures, disinclinations and lack of response. In either case, see Chapter Seven. Disagreements and unpleasantness in your personal relationship or household arrangements frequently upset your sexual capacities even if they do not cause frank arguments or general discontent. Chapter Eight tells you what to do. When a husband has trouble holding off until his wife feels ready for climax, Chapters Nine, Ten and Twelve should help to build her passion faster, or increase his staying power. If he cannot build his own excitement often enough to keep his wife satisfied, Chapters Ten and Twelve suggest effective measures.

STEP FIVE: *Conjoined Sexual Activity.*

After you have learned to please each other thoroughly with sexual activity in which only one partner takes a highly active role, you can move on to techniques requiring sexual movements by both partners at once. The wife should generally practice her new role first during episodes undertaken out of loving service rather than in the heat of passion. She must concentrate on making the proper motions and coordinating her rhythms with her husband's for a few encounters before she can perform these movements automatically, as discussed in Chapter Twelve. The standard husband-on-top position works out well, with the chair-borne astride posture a close second. The various rhythms discussed in Chapter Five and the climax-heightening techniques mentioned in Chapter Six help to keep fairly frequent use of the same positions from becoming boring.

You can work out a number of delightful sexual rhythms based on the slow male in-and-out motion with quicker female rocks or rolls. Add genital twitchings or spasms for extra fillips, rhythmic caresses of the breast or clitoris, buttock massage and other forms of exciting caress for keenly delightful interludes.

Sex at this stage becomes a rather vigorous and prolonged exercise for which most couples need to reserve their energies to some extent. Try to arrange complete privacy for occasional morning or daytime encounters or for a sexual climax to a pleasant evening out. Use part by part relaxation (pp. 87-8) for a half-hour rest break in the afternoon or early evening to refresh your energies for bedtime sex. Budget an hour or so of time and a complement of energy for sex, just as you budget a fraction of your resources for vacations and family fun. Spend time and effort on allurement, on a gradual build-up of excitement through sex play and intimate caress, on non-climactic sexual contact if necessary, and on full exploitation of every possible sexual delight. Hasty attentions and exhausted compliance make a poor foundation for compassionate couple growth.

STEP SIX: *Suit sex to the occasion.*

You need to vary your approaches and techniques to keep from getting tired of each other. Why not vary them to suit each episode to the occasion instead of for the sake of variety alone? When both of you are rested and firmly impassioned, a long build-up with playful retreats and varied advances leads naturally into vigorous conjoined activity in husband-on-top or chair-borne posture. When Mr. is fresh and Mrs. is somewhat weary, the wife's-heels-on-husband's-shoulders posture leaves him doing almost all the work while still contributing unique sensations to both. The reverse situation makes the wife-astride posture very suitable. When both partners feel weary or must not exert themselves because of illness, the crossed posture or husband-from-the-rear-while-lying-on-your-sides posture works out well.

Taking advantage of occasions to make a different approach also lends variety. The absolute privacy of a second honeymoon vacation might give you opportunities for abandoned sex play in the late morning or mid-afternoon when the children would certainly interrupt if you were still at home. The gay mood of a big celebration might set the stage for the specials discussed on pp. 106-9 or for a round of the most intense caresses discussed in Chapter Three. Sliding into sex play from the intimacies of a dance, a beach picnic or some other unusual occasion almost automatically leads you to a new approach. If you suit sex to all of these occasions, you will seldom have to seek variety for its own sake. However, don't let yourselves get into a rut in your sex life, even if the humdrum routine of your daily life seems to bring about the same type of couple communion night after night after night. Any time you find yourself in the same sex position twice in a row or discover that you have followed almost the same approach twice in the past four or five times, you should strive for changes. Have a glass of wine together in the bedroom, or feed each other sweetmeats if you don't like alcoholic drinks. Start your sex play with wife in husband's lap instead of lying in the bed. Dance to the radio in robe and negligee. Undress each other during sex play instead of waiting for lights out to start the game. Embrace each other face to face one night, with the husband behind the next night and the wife lying across his chest the next. These different starts will lead to different patterns without the constraint of planning step-by-step.

In choosing sex postures, the need for variety itself suffices to make any position in which you can consumate worth an occasional trial. Most couples find one or two positions give them the most pleasure, and tend to stick to those postures almost all of the time. The pleasure palls, not because they chose the wrong positions but just because the specific sensations stemming from those postures no longer give much thrill. If you use many postures, your favorites will give their full complement of joy each time you visit them again. See Chapter Four for a listing of possibilities.

STEP SEVEN: *Develop maximum sexual harmony and pace.*

After you have developed reasonably consistent, effective and varied means of satisfying each other, you no longer need to fear that deliberate exercise of knowledge, planning and technique will stilt your sex life. Like the polished dancer who glides through a planned routine with totally relaxed grace, you can use your sexual knowledge and skill without impeding your naturalness and response. At this point, each of you might find it worthwhile to assemble notes on your partner's responses. Write down which caresses seem especially exciting to your partner, which positions give the keenest delight, which measures seem to upset your partner or let passion sag. Then read Chapters One through Six and Chapter Twelve for further ideas to add to your notebook. Don't hesitate to discuss entries with your partner occasionally, perhaps even with demonstrations.

Deliberate planning and technique help match a husband's pace with his wife's passionate desire. Apply such methods as played-off preliminary climaxes (p. 153), episodes in which the man foregoes his climax (p. 154), genital twitching to bestir an extra female orgasm (p. 103), and seminal retention (p. 171) to produce couple harmony when the woman's desires exceed the man's. If the man's pace exceeds the woman's, she should not only acquiesce but should take pride in exerting every effort to increase male satisfaction. Her mate should appreciate her loving service with gentle caresses, unhurried pace and comfort-preserving movements at such times. The peculiar feminine enjoyment of bringing delight with one's body often builds into capacity for ardent interest and orgasm through the years if both parties play their proper roles, and actually gives most women intense satisfaction in itself (see Chapter Nine).

The last word.

Finally, when you have followed all seven steps to sexual success, never stop trying to improve. You can build sexual gratifications further and further as the years go by, if you continue to refresh your efforts with suggestions from this book. You can grow as a couple in conjugal capability through the years. You can cement your marriage thoroughly with sexual success.

INDEX

Dell Bestsellers